LIMINAL

Other books by R. A. Steffan

The Last Vampire: Book One
The Last Vampire: Book Two
The Last Vampire: Book Three
The Last Vampire: Book Four
The Last Vampire: Book Five
The Last Vampire: Book Six

Vampire Bound: Book One
Vampire Bound: Book Two
Vampire Bound: Book Three
Vampire Bound: Book Four

Forsaken Fae: Book One
Forsaken Fae: Book Two
Forsaken Fae: Book Three

The Sixth Demon: Book One
The Sixth Demon: Book Two
The Sixth Demon: Book Three

The Complete Horse Mistress Collection
The Complete Lion Mistress Collection
The Complete Dragon Mistress Collection
The Complete Master of Hounds Collection

Antidote: Love and War, Book 1
Antigen: Love and War, Book 2
Antibody: Love and War, Book 3
Anthelion: Love and War, Book 4
Antagonist: Love and War, Book 5

LIMINAL

R. A. STEFFAN

Liminal: The Morpheus Trilogy, Book One

This book is a work of fiction. Names, characters, businesses, organizations, places, events and incidents either are the product of the author's imagination or are used fictitiously. Any resemblance to actual persons, living or dead, events, or locales is entirely coincidental.

ISBN: 978-1-955073-75-2 (paperback)

For more information, contact the author at
http://www.rasteffan.com/contact/

Cover by Deranged Doctor Design

First Edition: October 2023

AUTHOR'S NOTE

I don't usually write books that are this shamelessly derivative. This time I did, because the second half of a certain television episode should have been an epic paranormal M/M love story but wasn't, and the writer was kind enough to use public domain myths as the story's underpinning.

Unfortunately, said writer was later revealed to be a truly horrific sexual predator, which was deeply disappointing on a number of levels. (Still only "alleged" at the time of this edition's update, but damningly corroborated by his own public admissions.)

Anyway, for obvious reasons, you won't find copyrighted or trademarked content from that television show here. For that, you'll want fan fiction, and I have no doubt there's a ton of it available. In this book, you'll find a story about the classical Greek god Morpheus and an immortal human embodying the Eternal Hunter myth, along with a celestial bet, a dastardly plot, and a slow-burn romance stretching more than eight hundred years.

Enjoy.

Table of Contents

ONE

The Night Lands

ONE OF HUMANITY'S greatest misconceptions about the Night Lands was that they lay in perpetual darkness—cloaked by despair and bereft of all warmth.

Morpheus sat with his father's eldest brother beneath the rustling branches of a massive oak, drinking wine plucked from the dreams of a Tuscan vintner. Diffuse golden light filtered through the leaves, painting the rough wooden tabletop in ever-shifting dapples. Beyond, a field of red and mauve flowers waved in the light breeze.

"You have to understand—it's built into them," Thanatus was saying. "Woven into their beings since they first started walking upright. I'm telling you, Morpheus—if you try making a human immortal, they'll go mad before the end of their second century."

Morpheus leaned away from his uncle's emphatic gesticulations, neatly avoiding the splatter of crimson wine that sloshed out of Thanatus' goblet. It wasn't accurate to say that he *disliked* these occasional spirited debates; merely that his style of argumentation was not always well matched with his uncle's. Where Thanatus was animated, Morpheus was self-contained.

Wooden, his brother Phantasos might say.

Just like the stick up his arse, Phobetor would doubtless have added.

Controlled, Morpheus might have retorted. *Perhaps you should both try it sometime.*

He met his uncle's night-black gaze, raising one skeptical eyebrow. "And yet," he argued, "I see the humans' dreams every night when they sleep. Always, they yearn for more time. They fear your approach with every breath."

The embodiment of death let out a bark of humorless laughter. "In dreams, they long for many things that would be bad for them in the waking world." He sat back, taking a deep draft of his wine before setting the goblet down on the table with a solid thump. "But here. I'll make you a wager, nephew. Choose a human. Any human. Pick one who dreams of eternal life. I will withhold my touch from them, and then we shall see what happens. If they make it two hundred years without begging for death, I shall concede that you have won. If they don't, you'll concede that I have won."

Morpheus pondered this proposal for a moment, twirling the thick stem of his goblet between slender fingers. "And the stakes?"

Thanatus seemed to think on it for some little time. "If I win, you will grant me a part of your realm to do with as I wish. Let's say… the lands between the River Lethe and the cave of Hypnos."

Morpheus narrowed his eyes. "And what would you do with such a bounty?"

Thanatus smiled, the expression baring a white slash of teeth in his dark-skinned face. "There are many who enter my realm in need of forgetting," he said, his expression sobering as he spoke. "Some are villains, and they deserve to relive their greatest regrets over and over for eternity. Others are victims, and the dreamless sleep of unbeing is all they crave."

Privately, Morpheus knew this to be true—and not just of the dead. There was a reason the hills in the Night Lands grew thick with opium poppies. He was not in a hurry to cede part of his lands to his uncle, but even so...

"You haven't said what reward I might gain, should I be the one to win your wager."

Thanatus tilted his head. "What reward would you wish for?"

Morpheus considered, letting the silence stretch between them. Eventually, he offered the kind of stakes that would ensure Thanatus' refusal.

"I would claim one unspecified favor from you at the time of my choosing," he said.

An unspecified favor from one of the gods was not the sort of thing for which one asked. Not even when one was also a god.

Thanatus scowled, the shadows around his eyes darkening and shifting until they seemed ready to crawl free into the air between them.

That's it, Morpheus urged silently. *Tell me to go to perdition, uncle, so we can both return to our work. This wager of yours is nothing but a farce.*

But after a few seconds, Thanatus' expression cleared. "That's no small request, nephew. Were I not so certain of the outcome, I confess I might be offended by your presumption. However, today

4

you will have your wager — even if the result is nothing more than a foregone conclusion. Choose your human champion and inform me when you have picked the one you want. We will visit them in the Sublunary as soon as you are ready to proceed."

Morpheus blinked.

Wait, what?

But Thanatus only lifted his now empty wine goblet in a final salute before he faded away into shadows.

Gone.

⸻◆⸻

Of course, Morpheus could have run after Thanatus and begged for release from the wager. He could have said it had all been in jest; that he hadn't really meant to agree to the terms. Instead, the God of Nightmares sat in his throne room, brooding, as he stared with an unfocused gaze at the mirrors lining the great stone chamber.

A slight susurration in the still air recalled Morpheus' thoughts to the here and now. Iridaceae flew in on silent wings, gliding down to perch on the arm of his throne. His owl familiar tilted her head curiously, luminous yellow-green eyes opening and closing in a slow blink as she took in the countless human dreams playing out along the walls. A moment later, reality twisted next to him. A petite, naked human woman curled hipshot on the arm of the throne, her demeanor aloof and birdlike.

"What are you doing, my king?" she asked in her haunting, sibilant accent.

"Nothing that concerns you," Morpheus replied.

Expectant silence reigned, piercing amber-green eyes pinning him with unblinking intensity.

Eventually, he gave in. "I made a bet."

Still no response.

"Possibly a foolish one," Morpheus added with a sigh. "I must find a human who will welcome the gift of immortality and not go mad afterward. Otherwise, I forfeit the land beyond the River Lethe to my uncle Thanatus."

Iridaceae gave an indignant squawk, shifting her shoulders jerkily as though resettling ruffled feathers. "My favorite tree is within those lands!" she complained. "There's a lovely nest of mice right in the roots!"

Morpheus attempted to convey censure via the medium of his stony expression. "Then I suppose you'd best hope I choose well."

With a disgruntled *hmph* noise, Iridaceae shifted back to her natural form and flapped away in a huff, leaving Morpheus once again alone with humanity's dreams.

Feeling unaccountably as ruffled as his owl, he forced himself to relax and sink once again into the collective unconscious of the Sublunary — the mortal world. It was the same primordial chaos that had spawned him… the flotsam and jetsam of sentience from which his entire being was formed. Navigating it was second nature, but he'd seldom plumbed these depths in search of a particular thing before.

He hadn't been lying to Thanatus. The sleepers' minds were rife with dreams and nightmares about death. Plagues were rampant in the human realm. War and disease felled entire families, entire villages. Men and women dreamed of death's approach and gasped awake, drenched in sweat, their mortal hearts pounding in fear.

This was not what Morpheus needed.

Choose a champion, Thanatus had told him. Somehow, the idea of forcing a human to fight this battle for him felt... *discomfiting*. Yet it seemed a champion was, indeed, what he required right now. He dove, immersing himself deeper in the maelstrom of memory and emotions, fears and aspirations.

Abruptly, he found himself standing in the shadowed corner of a peasant's hut as though he'd been drawn there by an invisible silken rope. A straw palliasse with its sheets soaked in fresh arterial blood dominated the room. On it, a woman writhed weakly, her face pale as a ghost's. A grim-faced midwife crouched at the end of the low bed, shaking her head.

Next to the dying mother knelt a man with plain brown hair and plain brown eyes. To Morpheus, he appeared utterly average in every way. The man was weeping openly, clutching at the woman's hand as he turned a begging expression toward the midwife.

"I won't lose them!" he said, though his voice was clogged with tears. "Do you hear me? *I will not.*"

"I'm sorry, sir," said the midwife. "But it's already too late. There's nothing more to be done."

"*No,*" the man whispered in a tone of sheer horror. Morpheus followed his gaze to the cottage door, where a figure in dark robes had entered, holding a scythe. Then the human's expression hardened, as did his voice. "No! *You will not have them!*"

A sword appeared in the man's hand with all the senseless illogic of dreams. He rose unsteadily to his feet, turning to block the shadowy figure's approach. Undeterred, the cloaked specter floated toward the sad forms of the dying mother and babe. With a wild cry, the man lunged forward, swinging his blade at the reaper's head. Before the blow could connect, the dream dissipated into mist, leaving only darkness as its dreamer jerked awake.

Morpheus blinked, recalling his consciousness to the seat of his power. Frowning at the wall of mirrors before him, he leaned an elbow on the arm of his throne and rested his chin on one hand thoughtfully.

"Well now, uncle," he murmured into the room's echoing emptiness. "One human champion to battle against Death, as requested."

TWO

1221 A.D.

THE ONEIRI WERE servants of the Night Lands, but not all of them served willingly. After returning from humanity's dreams to the physical plane, Morpheus summoned the nightmare that had masqueraded as Death into his presence.

It was an insubstantial creature, little more than a collection of shadows twisting in the space beneath the dais. Morpheus leaned back in his throne, considering it.

"Tell me of the dreamer who attacked Death with a sword," he commanded.

"Ugh. That brute?" The nightmare's voice was raspy and sniveling. "Aye, he's a scrappy one and no mistake. Nearly took my head off with that blade, he did."

"You don't have a head," Morpheus reminded it.

The shadows swelled, puffing up. "It's the principle of the thing, though, innit? Swinging a sword at the Grim Reaper himself? I ask you!"

The creature's outrage was palpable. Morpheus gave it a quelling look, staring down his nose from his elevated position. "Do not force me to ask you the same question twice. *Speak.*"

The nightmare's amorphous form deflated, slumping in on itself.

"Calls himself Hugh de Ferrers," it mumbled. "Lives in England, in a town named Bath — which is ironic since I don't think he's had one anytime recently. Spends his days nailing hot iron onto horses' feet, because humans are really strange sometimes. You don't never catch the horses dreaming about chopping my head off with a sword, now do you?"

"Thank you," Morpheus told it. "You are dismissed. Return to your work."

"Lucky me," said the nightmare, folding in on itself until it disappeared into the ether.

Morpheus tapped his fingers on the arm of the throne, considering.

Hugh de Ferrers.

A man who had recently lost his spouse and child. Perhaps he was not such an ideal champion after all. Many humans gave up their will to live after such an event. Just because this one had attempted to battle Death and save his loved ones, it didn't necessarily mean he would fight with as much spirit on his own behalf.

More investigation was in order.

The hours slipped past in the Sublunary, until night fell once more over the island containing the town humans called Bath. Morpheus once more lost himself in the chaotic currents of humanity's dreams, following the same thread that had drawn him to a grief-soaked cottage the previous night.

This time, the oneiri had been kinder to Hugh de Ferrers. His dreams had conjured a warm spring day and an idyllic landscape. The human sat leaning against the bole of an ancient tree. In his arms, he cradled a familiar, heavily pregnant woman against his body. She rested between his spread legs, her back against his chest.

She was not beautiful. Her face was long and thin, marked by strain… her hair lank beneath its wimple. Yet, when she looked up at the man behind her, her features lit with affection and love.

Morpheus had thought de Ferrers wholly unremarkable upon first viewing. However, the man's answering smile crinkled the edges of his eyes, making the plain brown of them sparkle in the evening sunlight.

The woman sighed, resting the back of her head against the crook of his shoulder. "I'm fair exhausted already, husband. and the babe won't come for another month yet, at least."

De Ferrers stroked a hand over her distended belly. "If I could take the labor from you, I would."

She slapped at his arm half-heartedly. "Don't be daft. I'd as soon take up blacksmithing as see you trying to birth a babe. Keep to your anvil and forge. Leave childbirth to those meant for it."

He chuckled. "I'm sure you'd make a fine farrier with a bit of practice."

"Hush, you. Maybe it'll be a boy, and you can train him up," said the woman.

Another beautiful smile lit his face. "I'd like that. Mind you, I'd like a girl just as much. But either way, I've got plans for the smithy. Big plans. There's so much I want to do."

The woman laughed softly, then winced and put a hand to her belly. "You always were a dreamer, husband. 'Head in the clouds, that one,' my mother used to say, back when you and I were children."

Morpheus' ears pricked at the word *dreamer*. After a moment's hesitation, he slipped deeper into Hugh de Ferrers' mind, taking care to cloak himself from the human's awareness.

It was a warm place. A *bright* place. Almost blindingly so. Even in sleep, de Ferrers' thoughts turned endlessly over plans, possibilities, aspirations, what-ifs and might-have-beens.

The churn of imagination ignited a familiar ache in Morpheus' chest—the inevitable reminder of the meaning that humans generated for themselves, and that he could only ever experience secondhand. He was the embodiment of the collective unconscious… of dreams and stories. It meant he had no dreams or stories of his own, only those winnowed from other minds.

Hugh de Ferrers had enough aspirations to last a thousand years.

Morpheus would give him that time. And if the Fates were kind, de Ferrers would take the gift and use it to win Morpheus' bet against his uncle.

◆

The city of Bath was a gray and chilly place on Easter morning in the year 1221 A.D., as the humans in the area currently reckoned their calendar. Morpheus walked along a wide, cobbled road with Thanatus at his shoulder, heading toward the massive Abbey where the men and women of the city worshipped their current god.

Morpheus did not feel the cold or the damp—not beyond a vague, philosophical understanding that mortals would find the conditions unpleasant. Neither he nor Thanatus had altered their preferred physical forms in any significant way, though they were both dressed in the local style.

Many of the humans looked at them with interest, a fact that probably had more to do with their rich clothing and relatively tall stature than their inhuman origins. Those same humans quickly lost interest, eyes going distant and sliding away from Thanatus in particular. Their minds might not register it on a conscious level, but the animal part of them registered *danger* and steered well clear of it.

"You're certain he'll be here?" Thanatus asked, already sounding bored.

"There are barely more than a thousand souls in this city, and today is one of their holy days," Morpheus said. "He should not be difficult to find."

The town's great church rose above them like something out of humanity's fantasies, stretching improbably toward the sky. Indeed, as they approached it, Morpheus could feel a faint tug toward the building's interior—the barest hint of a connection to the dreaming mind he had invaded such a short time ago.

The massive church doors leading to the nave had been thrown open. Inside, most of the population of the city milled about, separated from the priests in the chancel by an intricately carved wooden rood screen that allowed the commoners only tantalizing glimpses of the mysteries beyond.

The gods had always demanded opacity within their cults, but Morpheus found the current fashion of separating the worshipers from the priests—not to mention conducting services in a language none of the commoners spoke — moderately bewildering. He supposed it cut down on awkward questions from one's followers if nothing else.

Beyond the rood screen, a figure in white robes lifted a goblet of wine heavenward, holding it over his head and reciting bad Latin with an even worse accent. The commoners mostly ignored him, chatting among themselves and milling around the echoing space of the nave while the service droned on without their participation or input.

Thanatus leaned his head close, speaking softly. "Some of these people believe that viewing the elevation of the sacraments protects them from dying that day."

Morpheus cocked an eyebrow. "And does it?"

"No. But they do seem awfully surprised when I show up right after a Sunday Mass."

Morpheus pondered this. "I suppose it will protect at least one person here today… unless you wish to abandon this foolish wager."

Thanatus snorted. "*Abandon* it? And miss seeing the look on your face when your pet human comes crawling to you, begging for a release from immortality? Not likely, nephew."

With a frown, Morpheus turned away and began scanning the crowd using his slight advantage of height. The priests continued their pronouncements in Latin, increasingly butchering what had once been a perfectly serviceable language. He and Thanatus circulated among the bored worshipers, watching as some of them trickled into the chancel one at a time to receive their sacraments from the equally bored priest.

The tug on his awareness increased, and Morpheus turned to see a figure clad in brown work clothes skirting the edges of the crowd and slipping out of the cathedral.

"There," he said, touching his uncle's elbow and jerking his chin in the man's direction.

The pair followed their quarry out of the Abbey. For a large man, Hugh de Ferrers moved like a shadow as he skirted the outer wall of the structure, disappearing around the corner of one of its cruciform wings. Beyond lay an uneven, grassy field dotted with stones rising from the earth—some carved into the shapes of crosses, others simple and unadorned.

De Ferrers traveled a worn path winding through the graveyard with singular purpose until he came to a particular uncarved gray stone. He sank down next to it, hugging his knees to his chest and staring at the pile of dirt that had barely begun to sprout grass.

Morpheus grasped Thanatus' arm, halting him with a wordless shake of his head. They waited as the human sat unmoving, staring at the fresh grave, while inside the church, the priests continued their endless recitation of Mass.

Eventually, de Ferrers rose stiffly to his feet and wiped at his cheeks. He turned, only to freeze upon seeing Morpheus and Thanatus standing there, watching him. After a moment, de Ferrers jerked his gaze downward, staring at his feet rather than at them.

"M'lords," he muttered. "Did you need something?"

Morpheus stepped forward, gesturing for his uncle to stay where he was. The human's eyes were red-rimmed. Two high spots of color marred his cheeks, as though he were embarrassed to have been caught mourning his dead wife and child so openly.

Clasping his hands behind his back, Morpheus modulated his voice to the same low tone that soothed dreamers and controlled the dreams that visited them. "Hugh de Ferrers. My deepest condolences on your recent loss."

The man's gaze shot up at the mention of his name from the lips of a well-dressed stranger he'd never met before. Morpheus met startled brown eyes and inclined his head in acknowledgement of the oddity.

"Forgive me. I know we have not been introduced properly," he said. "But my companion and I have a proposal for you."

THREE

1221 A.D.

HUGH SCRUBBED AT his cheeks self-consciously, aware of what he must look like to the pair of fine lords watching him. In his experience, being singled out by the nobility never led to anything good. He had a feeling that being singled out *specifically by name* was far worse.

How could such men have possibly come to know of him?

He tried to study them without being too obvious about it, unsure whether they'd be the type to order someone flogged for failing to keep his eyes lowered. The slender one spoke prettily enough, all cultured manners and kind condolences. Hugh glanced up from beneath lowered lashes, taking in pale marble features that wouldn't have looked out of place on a statue of a martyred saint.

The man was beautiful in a way that didn't seem quite real — delicate and untouched by the sun. Probably never worked in the fields a day in his life, the lucky sod.

His companion had hung back a few steps while the first lord was speaking. The two were opposites in every way — one broad-shouldered and the other, slender. One luminous and white-skinned; the other as dark as oiled wood. And their eyes. The man who had spoken to him had eyes of a blue shade so intense it recalled the sky on a clear summer day. The dark-skinned man had eyes so black that the iris and pupil appeared indistinguishable in the gray morning light.

That night-sky gaze… Hugh couldn't have held it, even if he'd dared to try. His eyes and mind slid away like water beading off an oilskin. Trying to look at him for more than a flickering instant kindled an unpleasant tangle of emotions in Hugh's chest—fear, and disgust, and white-hot, irrational *rage*.

He dragged his attention away, staring once more at the toes of his boots while feeling mildly appalled by his reaction. His dear old mam had raised him better than that. *Just 'cause someone don't look the same as you, it doesn't mean you can act like you're better'n them*, she'd say. *Well — not unless they're Irish, of course. The only good Irishman is a dead Irishman.*

Hugh was pretty sure neither of the men were Irish.

A *proposal*, the slender one had said. He could guess what that meant.

"Am I to be conscripted?" Hugh asked, dreading the answer. He'd gained a decent reputation in the area as a farrier and blacksmith. Possibly that was how these two had learned his name. But the last thing he wanted was to be dragged from his smithy and forced to shoe horses for some nobleman's army in one of the pointless, endless wars between the barons and the throne.

"In a manner of speaking," said the pale lord.

"Look. I have a smithy to run," Hugh mumbled at his boots, achingly aware that he couldn't even plead the necessity of staying in Bath to look after his wife and infant child. "I can't be running around the countryside fighting someone else's battles."

Even as the words escaped him, he knew how foolish they had been. Men had been hanged for far less.

"Battles?" echoed the pale noble. "This proposal relates to nothing so mundane; I assure you."

The lord's voice was strangely hypnotic — a low, velvet murmur that made Hugh's insides want to curl up like a cat next to the fire, warm and purring. He chanced another look at the man. Black hair like eiderdown dipped in ink contrasted sharply with his radiant skin, and his expression wasn't unkind.

"Then what exactly is it? What do you want from me?" Hugh asked, still keeping his attention firmly away from the darker figure in the background. Even so, the hair at the base of his neck prickled with the awareness of a hart in the forest, trapped within the hunter's sights.

"It is a simple enough matter," said the slender lord. "Death has used you badly in recent days. I would beg your assistance in gaining revenge against its cruelty."

Forgetting his station completely, Hugh gaped openly at the nobleman. "Revenge... against *death*? How's that supposed to work, then?"

He'd heard whispers implying some of the local nobility had grown so inbred over the years that they'd lost their wits. He'd expect to see some other signs of it, though — a hunchback, or a clubfoot, or at the very least, buck teeth and a receding chin. Not this... *untouchable marble perfection.*

The faintest hint of a smile twitched at the edges of the stranger's lips, there and gone almost before Hugh registered it. "As I said, it is simple enough. You need only refuse death's advances for the next little while, thereby proving that it holds no dominion over humanity."

Hugh glanced helplessly over his shoulder at the fresh grave behind him, marked with its simple gray stone. Death's indelible legacy in his life, there for everyone to see.

"I don't understand, m'lord," he rasped, certain that he was the butt of some thoughtless joke.

"I know," the nobleman said. "However, you need not understand my request in order to accept it."

Hugh shook his head slowly back and forth. "But… I still don't know what you're asking of me."

Eyes of the richest indigo held Hugh pinned, unable to look away.

"I am asking you to live, Hugh de Ferrers. *Live*, and in doing so, prove that death holds no sway over you."

The dark man made a soft noise like a derisive snort, and Hugh felt his irrational anger flare once more, hot and bitter. He opened his mouth—unsure what words might emerge—but he didn't get the chance to find out.

"I will find you in one hundred years," the pale lord continued, ignoring his companion's rudeness. "No matter where you may roam, I will come to you on this holy day of Easter Sunday in the year thirteen hundred and twenty-one, so that you may tell me of your travels."

"But I don't *want* to travel," Hugh heard himself saying, as though he'd somehow forgotten how impossible the rest of the stranger's words were. "My life is here."

Behind him, the fresh grave mocked him silently.

"Then you will be quite easy to find," said the man. "I only need your consent."

The insanity of this entire conversation struck Hugh with its full weight. Grief stabbed at him anew, threatening to wet his cheeks with a fresh round of helpless tears. Abruptly, he couldn't stand to remain here under the scrutiny of these two richly dressed lords for another instant.

"Yes, fine, whatever you like," he said, hoping that agreement would convince them to go away and leave him alone. "A hundred years hence, on Easter Sunday."

The dark-skinned lord made another wordless noise. This one sounded like disappointment, or perhaps irritation. Hugh couldn't particularly bring himself to care.

"A hundred years hence," the pale lord agreed solemnly. "Until then—live well, Hugh de Ferrers."

Unable to help himself, Hugh glanced again at Agnes' grave—her body and that of their unborn child moldering in the cold ground of the churchyard. When he looked back, the lords were gone as though they'd never been.

"A hundred years, he says," Hugh grumbled. "What a load of old rot."

It was all complete nonsense, of course. Mostly, Hugh counted himself lucky that he had not, in fact, been conscripted into someone's army that day. His good fortune on that front lasted for the next twelve years, until the day that forces loyal to Baldwin III, the Count of Guînes, showed up at the smithy and pressed him into service.

The Count needed men to keep his horses shod, they told him. Baldwin had been tasked by King Henry to defend Monmouth against the foul machinations of Richard Marshal, the Earl of Pembroke.

Hugh didn't give two fucks about the conflict between a poncey king and an ambitious earl. Yet somehow, his lack of fucks didn't stop him ending up fifty miles from home, working day and night to keep a bunch of overburdened and underfed nags sound enough to carry armored knights as they attempted to hold off Pembroke's siege of Monmouth Castle.

That part was bad enough. But, when Baldwin lost so many men that someone shoved a sword hilt into Hugh's hand and screamed at him to fight for his life, things abruptly got quite a bit worse. He didn't see the enemy soldier who shoved a lance through his back—only the metal tip that erupted obscenely from his belly with an awful tearing sensation.

He thought, in the moment, that it should have hurt more than it did—especially when the weapon slid out again, leaving him with blood pulsing too fast and too red from his ruined stomach.

The pain came later. Followed, eventually, by blessed darkness.

When he next opened his eyes, he was surrounded by corpses, and someone was trying to tug his blood-soaked dagger belt and coin purse free of his limp body. The lad looting the corpses couldn't have been more than ten years old. He shrieked like a terrified cat when Hugh abruptly sat up, patting at his own abdomen with frantic movements as though to assure himself that nothing important had fallen out.

Somewhat improbably, nothing had.

The boy sprung away with Hugh's dagger belt in hand and sprinted for safety with his prize. Hugh—scrabbling clumsily to lift his tunic and shirt—was more preoccupied by the silvery scar, surrounded by crusted blood, that seemed to be the only remaining evidence of his mortal injury.

"Well, *shit*," he said to the raven-pecked corpses piled around him.

Unsurprisingly, none of them had any comment to make on the matter.

FOUR

1321 A.D.

THE NIGHT LANDS had been a restless place for several years by the time Easter Sunday in the year 1321 finally approached in the Sublunary. As the personification of humanity's dreams, Morpheus knew firsthand when widespread strife ruled the waking world. Huge swathes of the human population dreamt of hunger and cold—of banquets that crumbled to dust and rot the moment a hand reached out for the food... of hearth fires that guttered and gave off no heat.

Such discomfort was an abstract concept to a god. Morpheus could not perish for the lack of something like food or a warm hearth. If he wished to eat, he could conjure the finest of dishes from the dreams of mortals. If he wished for warmth, the merest flex of his power would alter his realm to suit his whims.

Humanity's dreams were also rife with violence. Mortals had always quarreled and warred with each other, but the last few centuries had been largely calm and prosperous compared to what came before. Now, it appeared their violence was no longer confined to nighttime flights of fancy.

Morpheus stepped sideways through the boundary separating the Night Lands from the waking world, following the slender thread he'd painstakingly teased free from the collective unconscious in preparation for his promised centenary visit to Hugh de Ferrers.

Last time, Morpheus and Thanatus had found the human among the graves of a churchyard. This time, his intended target was nowhere near a church—though an argument could be made that he was in the midst of a graveyard, nonetheless.

The dead and dying lay scattered on an expanse of mud-churned ground, surrounding the entrance to an unprepossessing manor house built of brick and stone with a timber roof. Moving among them was a figure, stooped with exhaustion, wielding a simple wooden spear.

Hugh de Ferrers shuffled from body to body, stopping at each one to drive the bloody point of the spear into the soft flesh of a throat. Occasionally, one of the bodies would twitch and gurgle, flopping like a fish for several seconds before going limp.

Irrational disappointment settled in Morpheus' chest like a lead weight. His champion against Death, his would-be knight defender, was spattered with drying blood, meting out the very curse that Morpheus had arranged to be withheld from him.

De Ferrers had expressed horror at the idea of being conscripted into a nobleman's army, and it was true that this place did not have the feel of a battlefield. It appeared to be someone's home, albeit a better class of home than the hovels of which the common folk dreamed. Some of the bodies on the ground were so small and slight that they appeared barely out of childhood.

Morpheus swallowed anger—as irrational as his earlier surge of disappointment—and stepped free of the cloak of shadows from which he had been observing his ill-chosen champion.

"This is how you choose to squander the gift you have been given?" he asked, appearing before de Ferrers in a swirl of rich fabric.

"*Christ!*" the human yelped, stumbling backward in surprise and nearly tripping over the wide-eyed corpse of a blond youth.

Morpheus regarded him, stony-faced.

De Ferrers managed to get his feet under him, gaping openly. After a moment, he snapped his jaw shut with a click. "It's… you're…" He shook his head and tried again. "You came. I didn't think you would." His eyes darted around the carnage. "This, uh, actually isn't a great time."

Morpheus raised an unimpressed eyebrow.

On closer inspection, the human looked terrible. His face was gaunt, his complexion an unhealthy gray. Dark circles underlined his sunken eyes. The hands holding the makeshift spear trembled.

"You have not answered my question, Hugh de Ferrers," Morpheus said, his tone resonant with power. "What crime did these people commit that would justify such a brutal sentence from one such as you, who have been tasked with resisting Death's dominion over mortals?"

De Ferrers' expression hardened. "Hoarding grain."

Morpheus did not release his gaze. "You would kill your fellow man over the seeds of plants?"

The human blinked at him as though his words made no sense. After a moment, he jabbed the spear point into the muddy ground and leaned on it. "Mate, in case you haven't noticed, *there's a famine on.* Has been for years. Don't talk to me about

Death's bloody dominion, because he's been reaping more souls than the farmers have been reaping wheat lately. Also, my name's not Hugh anymore. It's Hugo. As far as these people are concerned, Hugh was my grandfather's grandfather."

A shout came from one of the squat outbuildings flanking the manor.

"Hugo, come and see! There's enough grain in here to feed the village for six months, with more left over to plant!"

De Ferrers met Morpheus' gaze with tired brown eyes. "Look, I'm sorry I wasn't expecting you today, all right? I lost track of the year. Normally, I'd have some energy to spare for boggling over the fact that you haven't changed a whit during the last century, and that you apparently weren't bullshitting me back in 1221. But children are starving, and I've just helped a bunch of villagers massacre a fat baron's household so they can loot his granary. Like I said—not a great time."

Morpheus stared at him in frank disbelief. Had he just been *dismissed*? By a *mortal*?

"There's no polite way to put this," de Ferrers went on. "I don't know if you're fae, or a demon, or a vampire, or what. But you look like a nobleman—and in case you haven't noticed, noblemen aren't what you'd call popular around here at the moment."

"Hugo?" the voice from earlier called again, sounding closer this time.

De Ferrers didn't look away from Morpheus. "If you still want to talk to me, find me in a few hours. I hope you will, because an explanation for the last hundred years wouldn't go amiss. Right now, though, I've got—" He gestured around at the carnage. "—this mess to deal with."

Several people appeared, rounding the corner of the main house. "Hugo! Hey, who's that you're talking to?"

Stymied, Morpheus stepped back into the liminal space separating the Sublunary from the Night Lands. De Ferrers did an almost comical double-take at his apparent disappearance, but he recovered quickly.

"No one," he said. "So, how much wheat was the old hog sitting on, exactly? Can we fit all of it into the wagons and hand carts, do you think?"

⸻ ◆ ⸻

Morpheus watched from behind the veil of reality as his chosen champion assisted in the liberation of dozens upon dozens of rough burlap sacks from the dead nobleman's granary, each one plump and heavy with the spoils of the raid.

He was not accustomed to being disregarded, and certainly not by a human. Indeed, he wasn't entirely certain why he'd slipped out of the peasants' sight at De Ferrers' urging. It wasn't as though a ragtag group of mortals could harm him.

Rather than examine the disconcerting interaction any more deeply, he told himself that his caution stemmed from a desire to ensure that his uncle could not accuse him of cheating on their wager. While it hadn't been explicitly stated, it was understood that attempts by either of them to tip the balance in their favor by interfering in the human's life would not be tolerated.

Morpheus felt he was within his rights to check in on de Ferrers at the midpoint of the agreed-upon stretch of two hundred years—although he admittedly hadn't been prepared to rank lower in the human's estimation than a pile of fresh corpses and bags of grain. Nevertheless, he would not endanger the outcome of the wager by attempting to sway de Ferrers, either with dreams or with honeyed words in the waking world.

Eventually, the last of the carts and wagons departed with the grain. Meanwhile, the final few bodies were dragged into the nearby woods to be buried. The sun had grown low in the sky, and it occurred to Morpheus that he'd tarried here on the mortal plane for well over half a day. Watching de Ferrers, even though he had duties of his own in the Night Lands. Even though it was beneath him to await a mortal's pleasure like some sort of lowly servant.

"Go on, all of you." De Ferrers waved a hand at the collection of gaunt men laboring in the forest with him to bury the bodies. "It's getting late. I'll finish up here."

The largest of the men straightened with a grunt and wiped sweat from his forehead. "If you're sure." He looked at the shallow grave for a somber moment, then turned and clapped de Ferrers on the shoulder. "Today was a good day, Hugo."

De Ferrers made a noncommittal noise. He went back to filling in the end of the shallow trench, while the others gathered up their tools and headed out of the forest. When they were alone, Morpheus stepped from behind the veil, staring at the freshly turned soil.

The human stabbed his spade viciously into the remaining pile of dirt, dumping the shovelful of damp soil into the grave. "If you've got something to say, then say it," he said, not looking up. "Or, better yet, you could explain why I've stopped aging, and why I didn't die after taking a lance through the gut in 1235."

"You agreed to forego Death's attentions," Morpheus reminded him blandly. "And so you have, as promised. Now, tell me more of this famine."

De Ferrers stopped digging. "How can you not know about it? There hasn't been a decent harvest since the Year of our Lord, 1315!"

"Such things are not within my purview," Morpheus said.

"Not within your—" De Ferrers paused and shook his head, as though to clear it. "Who *are* you? *What* are you? Where are you from?"

Morpheus narrowed his eyes in warning. "The answers to those questions are not your concern."

After a long moment, the human let out a noise of disgust and went back to filling the end of the trench. "No," he said tightly. "You're right. My concern is five solid years of cold and rain causing the crops to fail. It's parents taking babies out into the woods and leaving them for the wolves to eat, so they can spare a bit more food for their older children in hopes of keeping *them* alive."

The shovel rasped, moving dirt from pile to trench in an angry rhythm. "It's cattle and sheep dying of disease and starvation, until almost none are left. It's people whispering about cannibalizing criminals and heretics because there's nothing else to eat. And meanwhile, the rich still have granaries full of wheat, waiting until the planting season when they can sell it for enough money to build their palaces out of pure gold."

"So, you killed them and took it." Morpheus eyed the grave with distaste.

The shovel faltered and fell to the muddy ground as the man holding it swayed. De Ferrers made a choked noise and staggered back a step, sliding down a sturdy tree trunk until he was slumped on the ground.

"There were thirteen people living in that manor house," he said hoarsely. "The baron, his family, and the guards he hired for the granary — some of them barely more than lads. But there are ten times that many people starving to death in the village. Why should thirteen people be allowed to glut themselves while more than a hundred starve?"

His pallor, which had been alarming before, turned ghastly.

Morpheus frowned at him. "When was the last time *you* ate?" he asked.

De Ferrers appeared to think on it for a few moments.

"Not sure. Don't really remember. Others needed the food more." He gave a rusty laugh, devoid of humor. "I mean, it's not like I can die from it, right?"

The frown deepened. "No," Morpheus agreed. "But you can still suffer."

De Ferrers scrubbed a hand down the length of his face, leaving a dirty smear behind on his cheek. "Yeah. I'd noticed, thanks."

"You are as deserving as any other human," Morpheus told him. "Did you not say that the wheat will feed the village through the summer, until the next harvest?"

Another pause, and de Ferrers nodded slowly. "It should."

"Then return to your home and accept your share of the bounty," Morpheus said.

The human looked up, meeting his gaze in the deepening dusk. "And if the crops fail again this year?"

Morpheus... didn't really have an answer to that.

"Perhaps they will not," he said eventually.

De Ferrers' brows drew together, as though he was attempting to determine whether the being who'd granted his conditional immortality might also have some insight into the future.

"Guess we'll just have to hope that's the case, huh?" he said. With a deep breath, he rose shakily to his feet, using the tree and the shovel for leverage. "It takes a lot of hope to make it through a century."

Mollified, Morpheus lifted his chin in acknowledgement. "I suppose it does. I trust you will marshal whatever hope is needed, for I will expect to see you on Easter Sunday in another hundred years."

De Ferrers looked at him from beneath a curtain of tousled brown hair. "Easter Sunday, 1421? Hmm. Demon or not, this time I almost believe you."

FIVE

1421 A.D.

THE DUNGEON WAS chilly and damp, rife with the smell of mildewed straw, piss, and festering wounds. At least some of the latter stench was coming from the bloody gash in Hugh's chest—a sucking wound that should have killed him. If his captors noticed that fact at some point before the injury inevitably healed, he wasn't certain what would happen next.

He was so fucking hungry, even though his stomach was a roiling mass of queasiness. *Hungry enough to eat a horse*, he thought… but in this godforsaken country, that joke wasn't even funny.

It was important that he avoid thinking about the battle. Had it only been yesterday? Yet again, he'd been conscripted into someone else's fight, dragged into King Henry's army and shipped across the channel to France. They were here to fight the Scots, he'd been told—because apparently, they couldn't just fight the Scots *in actual Scotland* like sane people.

He was to be under the command of the Duke of Clarence, they said—the same *idiot* nobleman who'd gone on to ignore the allied French and Scottish commanders' offer of a temporary truce through the Easter holiday. Instead, he'd decided to storm the enemy's position without warning or a workable plan. To top it off, more than half of the English archers had wandered off that morning to hunt game and plunder the nearest villages, and they were conspicuously absent when the order to attack had come down.

That strategy had certainly gone well, if by 'well' you meant that Clarence had been summarily killed by the enemy, along with several of his lieutenants. Meanwhile, most of the English forces that hadn't been slaughtered wholesale were now languishing in this benighted dungeon.

Including Hugh.

Fucking nobles.

He'd spent perhaps an hour distracting himself from his own agony by examining the workmanship of the iron shackle around his left ankle. It was crap—rough and marred by burrs—although the lock was a bit different than the ones he was used to seeing back in England, so that was interesting. The chain was pretty good. *Solid.* No gaps in the links, either.

The year was most certainly 1421, and he was fairly confident that today was Easter Sunday—unless he'd somehow lost a day to fever and despair. Unfortunately, the groans and cries of the other wounded men didn't have much in common with a church choir. Not that Hugh held much affection for churches these days; not after everything he'd seen in the last two hundred and twenty-odd years.

There were five other men in the cell with him, none of whom he knew by name. The youngest, barely more than a boy, had lost his battle against tears some time ago and was sobbing softly. The noise had become part of the background of suffering, but when it stopped, its sudden absence drew Hugh's attention outward from his own misery.

His cellmates all lay still except for the occasional sound of snoring. Evidently, they'd all managed to escape into slumber, a fact which sparked a deep sense of jealousy in him. A moment later, he felt an unexpected presence in the room. Looking up, he drew in a sharp breath when his gaze landed on two richly dressed figures — one delicate and pale as marble, the other as brown and unbending as polished oak.

On the positive side, Hugh's injured chest hadn't gurgled and bubbled when he gasped in shock. It must have finally closed up. On the negative side, he was still chained to the wall in a French dungeon, while the mysterious dark-skinned visitor stared down his wide nose at Hugh as though examining a pile of dogshit on the floor. Just as it had two hundred years ago, the man's presence elicited an irrational tangle of fear and rage in Hugh's chest.

"Hugo de Ferrers." The pale stranger, the man Hugh thought of as *his* stranger, stepped forward, raising a hand to keep his companion in place behind him.

"It's Hugh again," Hugh croaked. "Not Hugo."

The stranger's gracefully swept brows drew together. He really was quite unnaturally pretty, Hugh thought idly. Delicate as a bird's wing, and those *eyes* —

"It appears fortune has not favored you this Easter Sunday," the man said, not without sympathy. "I am sorry to see this."

Hugh reflected that, while there wasn't anything inherently *wrong* with possessing a grasp of the blindingly obvious, it also wasn't terribly help-ful.

"I don't suppose you've come to get me out of here? To pay my ransom or some such?" he asked hopefully, even though the idea made no sense. He'd only been captured the previous day. How could the stranger have received word so quickly?

"I'm afraid not." The stranger's sympathetic frown deepened.

Hugh's heart plummeted. This wasn't a res-cue—merely another brief centennial visit. Panic swelled inside his damaged chest. "Please… I don't want to be trapped in this godforsaken country! Just look at it! They eat *snails* here. Fucking *snails*! *Who does that?*"

"Now, don't be so hasty in your words, nephew," said the dark-skinned man. "You say you want to leave this place of suffering, Hugh de Fer-rers? I can arrange that."

The pale stranger's expression hardened into ice, and he turned a cold glare on his companion. "That is beneath you, Uncle."

The dark man gave a derisive snort. "On the contrary. That is the entire thrust of our wager, is it not? This human is suffering in body, mind, and spirit. Would you allow your base desire to prove a point to drive you to cruelty? I warned you they were not designed for this."

Hugh stared between the two, bewildered. "What… what *wager*? Are you going to help me get out of here or not?" An unpleasant itching sensation was beginning to take up residence beneath his skin... and it wasn't because of his festering wounds.

Hugh's stranger sighed.

"You will recall our agreement." His voice was soothing—rich velvet over night sky. "You were to live, and thereby prove that death holds no power over you. The escape my uncle offers is not an escape to freedom, but rather to the grave."

Hugh recoiled, scrabbling back toward the wall with arms and legs that didn't want to obey his commands. "You've come to *kill* me?"

The stranger's hard blue eyes pinned his dark companion. "That is not the reaction of someone seeking death's oblivion." The words were a sharp-edged blade.

Hugh's teeth ground together. "*What wager?*" he demanded, more forcefully this time. "You two! Neither of you have aged a day in two hundred years. And you... what? Made some kind of a *bet* about me? About whether or not I'd *beg for death?*" The words rose in both pitch and volume, but none of his fellow prisoners stirred. Beyond the walls and bars of this cell, the sounds of misery continued unabated.

"What have your two hundred years of life brought you?" the dark man asked. "What do you expect from the next two hundred years? Human life is comprised of suffering. I offer you its only solution."

I offer you...

Hugh stared at the mysterious figure, letting his feelings of rage and repulsion simmer—feeling out the sense of half-forgotten familiarity from long ago.

The memory of his beloved Agnes flashed across his mind's eye, pale and sweating as she labored in vain to birth their child. He remembered the phantom smell of blood, the clawing sense of helplessness tearing at his chest as though trying to break free of the cage of his ribs.

He remembered the same sense of sinking despair, paired with impotent anger, that he was experiencing now. The same feeling he'd experienced *both times* he'd been in the proximity of this man, with his oak-carved features and cold, black eyes.

Bile rose in his throat. Without conscious volition, he clambered to shaky feet. The iron links of the chain shackling him to the wall scraped against the stone floor as he staggered forward.

"*You*," he growled. The chain brought him up short, barely more than an arm's length from his target. "You took my Agnes. You took our baby. I remember you. I *dreamed* of you."

Hugh was barely aware of his pale stranger watching impassively from a few steps away. Meanwhile, the dark visitor's eyes seemed to swallow all the light in the shadowed cell. Or was that Hugh's own weakness, blackening the edges of his vision?

The man, if he truly *was* a man, lifted his chin. "Would you have preferred your wife to labor in agony for eternity, with a child trapped inside her, tearing her apart from the inside?" The question had no emotion behind it, only mild curiosity.

The rage that had been simmering beneath Hugh's skin erupted. He was still chained by one ankle… still out of arm's reach. His surroundings wavered in and out of focus. The sound of rushing blood pounded in his ears. Instinct propelled him to kick out, driving his foot violently into the man's balls.

It felt like kicking the castle's stone wall. The object of his anger didn't so much as flinch in response to the blow. By contrast, Hugh howled in pain and went down on his rump as his dizziness claimed him, the impact of arse against stone jolting up the length of his spine and exploding through the half-healed wound in his chest.

When his vision cleared, it was to find the dark man towering over him with an expression set in lines of cold fury.

"*You dare?*" His voice sounded too loud. Too deep. *Unearthly.* Shadows crept outward from his eyes. He took a threatening step forward, looming —

—and a pale hand descended on his shoulder, stopping him in his tracks.

The blue-eyed stranger insinuated himself between Hugh's crumpled body and a being that might well be the Grim Reaper.

"*No.*" The stranger's voice had also gained an unnatural depth of resonance. "You will honor the terms of the agreement, Uncle. Hugh de Ferrers does not die unless he explicitly asks to do so."

The shadows gradually receded. After a moment, Hugh's stranger released his grip.

The creature who might be Death stared down at Hugh, sending icy shivers of fear along his limbs. "Speak, then," he said. "Do you wish for death or not?"

A hatred as old as time itself swelled inside Hugh. He hawked and spat, the gob of bloody phlegm hitting Death's dark robes and sliding down the fine fabric.

"Go straight back to the devil, you foul creature," Hugh rasped. "Since that's clearly where you came from. I will never go with you willingly."

The Grim Reaper flinched back; a noticeably larger reaction than when Hugh had kicked him in the bollocks a few minutes ago.

"Hugh," said his pale stranger. "You have been a worthy champion. Thank you."

But Hugh did not reply. He rolled over to face the wall, curling around himself and refusing to look at either of them. The silence stretched for long minutes, until it was eventually broken by the stirring of his cellmates. Hugh peeked over his shoulder, but the two visitors were gone. Despair tugged at him once more, threatening to drag him down into darkness. Tears burned at his eyes, his chest catching on a sob. He pulled himself into a ball, hugging his knees as salty tracks dripped down his cheeks.

This will pass, he chanted silently. *It won't be forever. Better days will come.*

◆

Eventually, exhaustion pulled Hugh into restless sleep. Dreams followed, and he found himself back on a battlefield. All of the battlefields he'd seen in his unnaturally long life, in fact, muddled together into a nightmare landscape of blood and death and screaming.

He stared at the sword in his hand, only to discover that he was holding a wooden stick. It was barely more than a twig. Arrows rained from the sky. Beside him, Philip—a fresh faced farmer's son who'd once pressed him up against the wall behind the inn they were using as a barracks, kissing him as sweetly as any maiden—fell with a cry, three arrows protruding from his throat, leg, and torso.

Hugh whimpered and dropped the useless twig, curling up next to the twitching corpse and covering his head with his arms as the battle raged around him. He could block out the sight, but the deafening sound of clashing armies still reached his ears.

And then, abruptly, it was gone.

"Hugh?" A feminine voice asked, breaking the sudden silence.

Fingers stroked through his hair. He was no longer crouched on a battlefield, but rather he was lying on his side with his head resting on a soft thigh. Birdsong twittered in the gentle breeze, a melodious counterpoint to the quiet rustling of branches. The sound of children playing filtered to him from the distance.

"Easy, now," Agnes said, her fingers carding through Hugh's tangled locks. "You had a nightmare. All is well. You should try to get some more rest, my love."

Hugh caught his breath, blinking his eyes open to the sight of a peaceful glen dappled with midday sunlight. Serenity settled over him like a comfortable cloak, banishing the half-forgotten terrors of the bad dream. His hand lifted, catching Agnes' callused fingers and pulling them to his lips, where he pressed a soft kiss to her knuckles.

Still holding on to the physical connection, he rolled onto his back in the lush grass, looking up at his wife's familiar face. A grin of happiness crossed his features, and he squeezed her hand, bringing it to rest over his heart as all his cares faded away.

"Rest, yes," he said. A wide yawn nearly split his face in two. "I *am* feeling very tired."

Agnes smiled down at him. He blinked his eyes as the dapples of light shifted across them, and as he did, his wife's familiar face seemed to melt into something sharper for a flicker of a moment — something more masculine, almost hawklike. The impression of depthless blue eyes and dark hair as soft and wild as eiderdown brushed against his awareness, but it was gone so quickly he was sure he'd imagined it.

Before he could wonder about the odd illusion, warm darkness cradled him, making him forget about everything except deep, dreamless sleep.

SIX

1521 A.D.

MORPHEUS WAVERED for a humiliatingly long time over the prospect of visiting his erstwhile champion on Easter Sunday of 1521, as it was reckoned in the Sublunary.

On the one hand, he no longer had cause. Thanatus had conceded the wager between them, albeit with ill grace. Just as Morpheus would have been required to follow through by ceding his lands if Thanatus had won, his uncle would now be required to grant Morpheus an unspecified favor at a future time of his choosing.

Not that Morpheus had any intention of rubbing his uncle's face in the loss. There was nothing Thanatus could grant that he needed or desired. At least, there was nothing which couldn't be acquired more easily through some other means. What use was a favor to a god? Asking for those terms had been an act of insolence more than anything else. Morpheus had hoped to turn his uncle away from the wager with his presumption, nothing more.

Regardless, now that he had won, his reason for visiting Hugh de Ferrers on the earthly plane no longer existed. And yet...

For years after discovering the human languishing in a dungeon, Morpheus had tasked the oneiri with easing his dreams. That first night, he had visited de Ferrers in sleep himself, steering his nightmares into something soothing. It seemed the least he could do, considering the way they'd parted. An observer might have cause to believe that Morpheus owed the man a debt. Certainly, it would have been churlish to deny him the balm of Morpheus' own domain when the conditions of his waking life were so trying.

After a dozen years or so had passed in the Sublunary, the oneiros Morpheus had ordered to look after him reported that nightmares no longer threatened the human's mind every time he closed his eyes. Morpheus had quietly looked in on the human realm, discovered de Ferrers safely returned to his native land, and thought little more about it.

But as their next centenary mark approached, he wavered. Surely it would only be right to visit the human and inquire if he still wished to live. *Hugh de Ferrers does not die unless he explicitly asks to do so,* he had told Thanatus. That had been part of the terms, and the fact that the wager itself was over did not release Morpheus from his responsibility for de Ferrers' continued existence.

Irritated, he clenched the arms of his throne and pushed upright. This was ridiculous. He would visit the man. Assuming de Ferrers didn't spit in Morpheus' face as he'd spat on Thanatus' robes in the dungeon, Morpheus would ask if he still wished to live. If he did, that would be the end of it. If he didn't, Morpheus would inform his uncle that his services would be required after all.

It was but a minor thing.

"Iridaceae," he called.

A moment later, his familiar swooped into the throne room in her owl form, fluttering to rest on his outstretched arm. Her talons dug into the sleeve of his robe as she settled herself onto her perch. Large eyes blinked at him as she trilled a wordless question.

"We are traveling to the Sublunary for a brief visit," he said. "It is possible I will need you to relay a message to Thanatus, here in the Night Lands."

Her head tilted curiously in response to his words, but then she fluffed up her feathers and began preening one wing, unconcerned.

Morpheus lifted her to perch on his shoulder instead of his forearm, staring into the myriad of reflecting mirrors on the far wall as he separated the strands of humanity, seeking out one that he had followed before. Mentally taking it up, he slipped sideways through the veil.

He emerged into a sunlit morning. Iridaceae — every bit as nocturnal a creature as her master — gave an unhappy warble in reaction to the brilliant light.

"Wait here for me," he told her, indicating a large tree nearby. She flapped away, disappearing into the tangle of shadowed branches near the center.

They were in a relatively open area, surrounded by the bustle of a decently sized city in the distance. The structure in front of Morpheus was large, but shabby. A warehouse, perhaps, or a generously sized agricultural building of some kind. It had an air of long abandonment, the impression marred somewhat by a confusion of fresh footprints pressed into the muddy track leading to the closed double doors. That, combined with the faint murmur of voices filtering out from inside, indicated occupation on this holy day for the humans.

Morpheus slipped through the veil and emerged inside, cloaked by shadows of an entirely natural variety. From his dark corner at the back of the building, he observed perhaps two dozen humans seated uncomfortably on low, rough-hewn benches arranged in the central space.

Beams of sunlight pierced through holes in the ancient roof, illuminating the worshippers. A lone figure stood before them, reading in English from a thick, leatherbound book cradled in his hands.

Morpheus scanned the backs of heads, feeling his way simultaneously through the ether for the faint thread of connection to his target. His gaze alit on a brown-haired figure sitting attentively in the back row. That attentiveness was a façade; Hugh de Ferrers' mind had wandered to daydreams.

Such flights of daytime fancy were more in the purview of his brother Phantasos, but Morpheus caught a hint of wistfulness and a half-formed image of the cathedral in Bath, just before a flash of his own visage appeared. The human shifted on his uncomfortable seat, his flight of memory cutting off abruptly.

Interesting.

Morpheus had assumed that after 1421, de Ferrers would have little desire to meet with him again. He'd been understandably upset upon discovering that he'd become a plaything of the gods—if that was how he even saw Morpheus and his ilk.

The scene inside this abandoned structure certainly had some notable differences than the service three hundred years ago in Bath. It was small. Intimate, with a marked air of informality as the preacher read stories in a language his listeners could actually understand.

The gathering appeared to be wrapping up, ending with a series of prayers spoken collectively by the entire congregation. Morpheus waited, watching as the small crowd rose and broke up into twos and threes, talking quietly of casual topics. When de Ferrers finally made his farewells to the people to whom he'd been speaking and headed for the doors, Morpheus slipped through the ether, reappearing outside.

De Ferrers stopped abruptly, stared at him for the space of a handful of seconds, and then started walking again. Morpheus gestured for Iridaceae to attend him. She flapped down to perch on his shoulder, and when she was settled, Morpheus joined the human, walking at his shoulder along the dirt track.

De Ferrers shot the owl a suspicious sidelong glance, but he kept walking. "Didn't know whether to expect you or not after last time," he muttered after the silence stretched to uncomfortable lengths.

He was dressed well but not ostentatiously, in a loose linen chemise, doublet, jerkin, and hose. The terrible pallor evident during Morpheus' last two visits was absent, replaced by a healthy glow. He appeared, to Morpheus' mild satisfaction, well rested.

"This century appears to agree with you," Morpheus observed neutrally.

De Ferrers snorted. "Guess you could say that. The Scots and their French puppet masters eventually shipped me back to England along with the rest of the prisoners who managed to survive that long. I decided shortly thereafter that I was done being a pawn of noblemen, clergymen, and all the other leeches who think they can play dice with the common people's lives."

The human shot him another sidelong glance, this one decidedly pointed.

Morpheus, wisely, did not reply.

When it became obvious that he did not intend to rise to the bait, the human let out a heavy sigh. "Anyway, I started looking for other people who were sick and tired of the world's bullshit, and who were trying to do something about it. Stumbled across some followers of John Wyclif not long after I got back from France, and, well—" He gestured to the building behind them. "—here I am."

Morpheus contemplated his words, making connections. "You have become part of a religious sect? One that conducts its gatherings in secret?"

The human grunted. "I'm mostly here for the politics. Wyclif had some good ideas, mixed in with some fairly daft ones. I do like that he translated the Bible into English, though. It's a lot less boring when you can understand the stories."

"What sorts of ideas?" Morpheus asked, mildly intrigued by the shift and pull of human religions as they stretched across time.

De Ferrers turned to look at him properly as they walked, perhaps to assess his sincerity in asking the question. He seemed satisfied by whatever he saw.

"Well, he was against the clergy holding positions of temporal power, for one. He argued for keeping the Church and the Crown separate, as a means to prevent corruption. And, more importantly to me, he thought Christians should avoid engaging in wars and battles. I'm all for that part, unsurprisingly."

Morpheus remembered the man's nightmare of the battlefield. He nodded. "I see."

"As far as the daft stuff," de Ferrers went on, "he's got some really odd ideas about nuns. He's also firmly against exorcisms, which, uh, might be something you care about."

Iridaceae squawked, and Morpheus raised a slow eyebrow.

De Ferrers shrugged. "Just saying. Let's see… oh, yes. He was against requiring the clergy to remain celibate. But not because that's a crappy thing to ask of someone. No… he was convinced it was driving them to widespread sodomy. Because apparently the man never met a sodomite outside of a seminary," he finished with a soft, derisive snort.

The recent human obsession with who put what body part into what orifice was a source of bewilderment to all who dwelt in the Night Lands, and Morpheus was no exception.

"Those in power are still concerning themselves with such things?" he mused. "How tiresome. It seems only yesterday that any nobleman worth his salt kept a catamite as well as a wife."

De Ferrers came to an abrupt halt on the track, and when Morpheus turned, it was to find him craning around as though to search for potential eavesdroppers. The human huffed and hurried to catch up. The tips of his ears had gone red.

"You can't say things like that where anyone might hear." As Morpheus watched, his cheeks colored as well.

"I assure you, I can," Morpheus said, with mild irritation. "What a bizarre thing on which to fixate."

The human continued to stare at him. "… Right. So, maybe that's the prevailing opinion in the second circle of Hell, or wherever you're from—but up here, it'll get you in trouble if you're not careful."

Irritation turned to amusement. "You think me a demon?" On his shoulder, Iridaceae gave a quiet hoot of owlish laughter.

De Ferrers eyed the bird. "Got no clue what you are, mate. For that, you'd have to give me something beyond cryptic horseshit and bland platitudes."

Morpheus stiffened, abruptly becoming aware that he had strayed from his purpose here. "Then I will ask you a question instead. Do you still wish to continue your life in the mortal realm?"

The human's expression darkened. "Now that your little wager with the Grim Reaper is over, you mean?"

Morpheus narrowed his eyes. "Precisely."

"I'll tell you exactly what I told him last time, right after I kicked him in the balls." De Ferrers stopped, and Morpheus turned to face him. "Go to the devil, because I'm never choosing death willingly."

Morpheus' growing anger swirled together with a hint of something that might—oddly—have been relief. "Then I will leave you to your human life."

"Wonderful," de Ferrers said. "Guess I'll see you in 1621 then."

Morpheus did not reply, stepping instead into the shadows behind the veil and disappearing. The human's face faded from view, replaced with the wall of mirrors in his throne room in the Night Lands.

"Insolent creature," he murmured.

Iridaceae gave a low warble of amusement.

<hr>

Irritation did not absolve Morpheus of the debt he owed Hugh de Ferrers, however. Although the man had apparently found a sense of serenity after the many horrors he had seen and experienced in the mortal realm, Morpheus continued to task the oneiri with watching over his rest.

Less than a week had passed in the Sublunary when the dream-servant responsible for the task slipped into the throne room in a wash of rose-scent and soft pastel light.

"Um... your majesty?" it began, in a voice like the sound of distant bells.

Morpheus scowled at it. "Yes? What is it?"

It squirmed uncomfortably. "There's... uh... I guess you could call it a *situation*?"

"Speak in something other than riddles, please," Morpheus said, not feeling overly burdened with patience.

"It's the human," said the dream. "The immortal one, I mean. The one you told me to look after."

"What about him?" Morpheus asked.

The creature's squirming grew more intense. "It, um, might be easier to just show you? Because, well, I know I'm supposed to keep him happy… but frankly I don't get paid enough for this kind of shit." The final words emerged in a tumbling rush.

At the end of his tolerance, Morpheus waved a hand at one of the mirrors, calling up his connection to Hugh de Ferrers' sleeping mind. As the image coalesced, Morpheus leaned back in his throne rather abruptly.

Within the mirror, a vision of Morpheus himself lay naked, sprawled on a bed piled with furs—a vision of languid sexual debauchery.

"Oh," he said, rather blankly. "I… see."

SEVEN

Dream Interlude I

TO HIS CREDIT, de Ferrers had made a decent guess at what lay beneath the rich clothing Morpheus manifested for his centenary visits to the Sublunary.

Many of those who called the Night Lands home prided themselves on exceptional height or breadth of shoulder, muscular strength or athletic prowess. Morpheus found lithe elegance of form more pleasing. His current appearance was what it had been, more or less, since the Greeks had dubbed him Hypnos and claimed him as one of their gods. Only the blue of his eyes was a relatively recent affectation. While taller than the majority of the half-starved peasants scratching in the dirt of the Sublunary, he was not freakishly so. And although it had pleased him to sculpt defined muscles covered by only the barest layer of fat and pale skin, he was slender rather than brawny.

To see himself almost—but not quite—as though viewing his reflection in an earthly mirror was… odd. Doubly so, since he wasn't in the habit of writhing naked in front of random reflective surfaces.

"You may go," he told the thoroughly disconcerted oneiros that still floated in the corner of the throne room. "I will deal with this human myself."

The dream-servant had apparently been hoping for such an outcome, because it departed with a turn of speed seldom exhibited by such creatures.

Alone, Morpheus stared at the mirror for longer than he would have cared to admit, dithering. Something about the situation left him unsettled. Eventually, it occurred to him that it might be the novelty of seeing himself within a mortal's dream. Night after night, they dreamed of everything and nothing—but never of *him*. How could they? He *was* the collective unconscious... the clay from which their minds shaped the desires and fears manifested within dreams. One could not form a statue representing the very clay used to sculpt it.

While Morpheus had visited the Sublunary occasionally both before and since his wager with Thanatus, the minds of those mortals with whom he had contact always seemed to shy away from the fact of his existence. Those who followed the old beliefs knew him only as an abstract concept—the God of the Sleeping Mind.

There was absolutely nothing abstract about Hugh de Ferrers' dream.

He tilted his head, attempting to decide if mortal bodies could actually bend far enough to achieve the position in which de Ferrers had placed him. With no answers—and the nagging sense of being about to embark on a course of action that he would later come to regret—Morpheus let his consciousness sink into the maelstrom of dreamers.

As he had done on a handful of occasions before, he slid through the confusion in search of a single mind. Even as he did so, it was with the knowledge that he hadn't yet chosen a specific course of action relating to de Ferrers' frankly unnerving dream.

The room in which he coalesced was not something drawn from the human's personal experience, that much was clear. It was a common man's fantasy of a castle—a fairytale creation of gold and marble and splendid arches, furnished with every comfort mortal wealth could afford—centering around a magnificent four-poster bed of rather unlikely size. Morpheus lurked beyond the edges of the human's awareness, still at a loss as to the appropriate course of action.

In the absence of the flustered oneiros, the dream would soon twist itself into something unrelated as de Ferrers' mind wandered through the Night Lands, untethered. Already, the edges of the palatial bedroom were beginning to blur, a field of waving grain visible through one translucent wall.

Unsure where the impulse had come from, Morpheus raised a hand and stabilized the dream, directing it back to the path de Ferrers' subconscious mind had originally laid out. His eyes lingered without his conscious volition on the naked manifestation of himself. Aside from the obvious salacious nature of the scene, he was somewhat bewildered by how pleasingly the human's mind had painted him.

There was a softness, a *pliancy* to his form that Morpheus was quite certain did not exist in reality. He lay sprawled on his back among a profusion of rich furs and silk cushions, one leg hooked over the human's shoulder as de Ferrers drove into him with powerful thrusts.

Idly, Morpheus wondered how true to life de Ferrers had painted *himself*. Some humans dreamed themselves stronger, some weaker. Some manifested fantastical physical beauty, some dreamed themselves ugly and twisted.

De Ferrers' face was certainly reflective of reality, caught forever at the age when Thanatus had turned away from him in 1221 A.D. His body seemed… plausible, for a mortal whose muscles had been honed at a blacksmith's anvil. The fact that his right bicep and forearm were more developed than the left—from regularly wielding a heavy hammer right-handed—further reinforced the verisimilitude of the dream image. Broad shoulders tapered to a waist that was solid as opposed to trim. Muscular buttocks flexed with each punishing stroke into the receptive body beneath him.

"Beautiful *bastard*," de Ferrers growled, his right hand wrapping around Morpheus' cock and pumping in time with the movement of his hips. "Talking about fucking *catamites* outside of a fuck-ing *church* on Easter *fucking* Sunday."

The dream-image of Morpheus threw its head back and keened, as de Ferrers punctuated the words with a series of sharp thrusts.

"Won't tell me what you *are*—" Another sharp snap of the hips. "Won't tell me why you chose *me*—" And another. "Won't tell me what the hell I'm supposed to *do*. What the *hell* am I supposed to *do now*?"

Morpheus' dream image arched and cried out, seed pulsing from his prick in thick, messy ropes that painted the smooth white skin of his belly and chest with pearlescent trails. He felt an echo of the clench and release of pressure deep within the cradle of his pelvis. His vision wavered between a view from the corner of the room and a view of de Ferrers' face — flushed and tormented — gazing down at him from close range. With a start, he realized that he'd unconsciously slipped partway into the human's dream.

He jerked himself back, recentering his essence in the position of observer rather than participant, just as de Ferrer's groaned and spilled into his dream-form, powerful hips losing rhythm.

A pregnant silence descended over the scene, broken only by the combined sounds of heavy, shuddering breathing. De Ferrers disengaged, removing dream-Morpheus' leg from his shoulder with gentle care. The human flopped onto his back, lying stretched out beside the vision he'd conjured. Both figures stared up at the emerald-green canopy draped over the improbably large and ornate bed.

"You could at least have told me it was a wager," de Ferrers said, into the increasingly heavy atmosphere. "You could've warned me what was going to happen to me."

Dream-Morpheus drew breath as though to speak, though it would not be truth. It would only be whatever de Ferrers wanted to hear… or feared to. In his shadowed corner, Morpheus jerked a hand up, swiping it across the post-coital scene in an abrupt, almost angry gesture — catapulting de Ferrers back to the waking world, where he would doubtless need to launder his sheets.

"Prophecy is not my function," he said to the blank grey swirl of nothingness left behind. "And the wager was not my idea."

EIGHT

1621 A.D.

LOOKING BACK ON IT, Hugh's decision not to attend Easter Sunday service in 1621 had been a mistake. Yes—that was definitely where he'd gone wrong. That, and not getting out of Ipswich sooner, of course.

He was an idiot. People left from Ipswich's port to travel to the New World in droves. Hugh could have gone at any time, starting yet another new life in a far-flung land. It wasn't as though blacksmiths weren't in demand in New England, either. It was such an obvious thing to have done, and yet, he hadn't done it.

Life had been too comfortable these last couple of decades, and Hugh had allowed himself to become complacent.

However, complacency hadn't been the reason behind his decision to stay home on Easter morning. Yes, it was partly because he'd become disillusioned with the Church—and religion in general—after watching the grand visions of reform across the last hundred years come to naught. Mostly, though, he wasn't willing to risk his stranger showing up during the middle of the service and talking about catamites again.

A century later, and that particular bit of madness was still lodged in his memory like a burr beneath a saddle blanket. Heavens preserve him, there had been times he thought he might go mad with it. Truly, if smiting was within the stranger's powers, some of Hugh's dreams across the intervening years would have seen him summarily smote, rather than irrationally smitten.

How could a creature be so infuriating, yet so alluring at the same time? It simply wasn't fair.

Anyway, that was why Hugh was sitting in his comfortable cottage, rather than a pew—sipping small beer as he waited for his stranger to appear, and ignoring, with difficulty, the urge to go for something stronger. Midday was already approaching. There hadn't been a specifically set time for the stranger's arrival during their previous once-a-century meetings, so Hugh didn't give much thought to the time beyond a vague awareness that the town's churchgoers would be returning home by this hour.

The sound of fists pounding violently on his rickety front door nearly made him knock over his beer. He jerked upright from his tiny table, steadying it with both hands as it wobbled under the unaccustomed abuse.

A wild thought came to him. Was it his stranger? Was the man in trouble somehow?

But no. That was unthinkable. His stranger appeared in silence, as though from nowhere. Picturing him thumping on a door hard enough to break it down made about as much sense as imagining an ancient oak tree growing wings and taking flight, ripping its roots from the ground as it rose into the air.

Which meant—

Angry shouts joined the pounding. Before Hugh could decide on a reasonable course of action, the abused doorframe splintered. The door crashed inward to smack against the shelves on the wall next to it, rattling the timbers.

"There he is!" cried a voice.

Several others chorused, "*Get him!*"

Hugh gaped as neighbors and acquaintances and tradesmen he'd known for years poured into his home, swarming toward him. Most of them were armed with rude weapons — tools and bits of wood brandished like clubs. They were on him in a trice, almost before his pounding heart caught up with events. Hobbled both by superior numbers and his desire not to injure people he'd known for years, he abruptly found himself pinned on his stomach on the cobbled floor. Rough stone scraped his cheek.

"What are you *doing?*" he tried to ask, even though a small corner of his mind had already guessed.

It was drowned out by the excited cries of the mob.

"Search the house!"

"Find his books! Look for strange symbols!"

"Get his clothes off — look for a witch mark!"

Nausea roiled in Hugh's gut. Twenty-two years. He'd stayed here too long. Changed too little.

"I'm not—" he gasped, only to be cut off by a knee pressing into his kidney.

"Shut yer hole, witch!" grated old Tom Hartle, the miller.

Rough hands yanked at his clothing, tearing seams and ripping laces. Hugh squeezed his eyes shut, fear and humiliation flooding him like water and wine swirling together.

He couldn't die, *he couldn't die*. And what might they do to him, that he would have to live through? Witches were hanged. They were drowned. They were burned at the stake. His breath caught, the air trapped and frozen to ice inside his lungs.

"I'm *not* —" he tried again, as fingers tore at his loose linen undershirt and smallclothes. But… what if he was?

He was four hundred years old. He'd met the Grim Reaper. He'd spat on the man and kicked him in the bollocks, for god's sake. His mysterious stranger had granted him immortality on a *bet*.

"He's got lots o' books here," cried Mary Williams, the baker's daughter. "Some of 'em have got weird symbols on the front!"

His books. His beloved books, gathered from his travels over the course of centuries. His jaw clenched tight as the last of his clothing was pulled away, leaving him naked on the cold floor.

"Rector says maybe he uses his forbidden books to summon demons," drawled one-eyed Henry from the tavern. "Made a pact with the devil to keep him young, while everyone else turns old and gray. Probably drank baby's blood to seal it!"

"If so, he'll have a mark," Tom Hartle said grimly, hauling Hugh up from the floor. More hands grabbed him, restraining him. "Witch's mark. Just hafta find it is all."

"Get him outside!" someone shouted. "We'll drag him to the church!"

Hugh bit back a sob of terror, knowing how it would go. They'd shave his body of hair… find a mole or a scar or a wart… call it a witch's teat and start driving pins into him to see if he could feel pain.

Why hadn't he left when he had the chance? God save him, *why hadn't he left before they started suspecting his secret?*

"Outside with ye," Hartle ordered, gesturing sharply toward the remains of the front door.

His captors dragged him forward...

... And stopped short upon seeing the figure in a dark cloak blocking the broken doorframe, the slender form silhouetted against the brilliant sunlight outside.

Hugh choked on nothing, his knees threatening to give out at the sight.

Mary Williams screamed. "It's the devil! *It's the devil!* He just appeared out of nowhere! I saw it happen!"

Several people whipped out rough wooden crucifixes, holding them up as though they were weapons. Gasps and shouts echoed around the cottage.

Naked and bruised, Hugh stared in combined hope and horror as his stranger stepped inside, pale blue eyes sliding over the crowd of frightened townsfolk with disdain until his gaze fell on Hugh.

Hugh tried to draw breath—to beg for help, to tell him to run... he wasn't sure.

A small furrow formed between dark, elegant brows, barely visible in the dim light of the cottage interior. The stranger lifted one arm in a smooth gesture, and the hands holding Hugh fell away. Everyone in the cottage except him collapsed to the ground, makeshift weapons clattering to the cobble-stones as they slipped from nerveless fingers.

Hugh stumbled back a step, nearly tripped over Tom Hartle's unmoving body, and went down on his knees with a jarring thud. His breath came in great, whooping gasps, too loud in the sudden silence.

The stranger peered at him in apparent consternation. "What happened here, Hugh de Ferrers? Why were these people attacking you?"

That soothing, velvet-over-steel tone nearly reduced Hugh to tears. He had to dig his fingernails hard into his palms to swallow them back.

"Th-they thought I was a witch," he said, his voice a hoarse croak. "I've been here too long. I don't look old enough. They think I sold my soul to a demon and that's why I don't age. They would have b-burned me, or drowned me, or hanged me."

His limbs were shaking uncontrollably. His body had gone as cold as though he'd been standing in freezing rain for hours. He hugged himself tightly, too aware of his nakedness.

The stranger tilted his head, birdlike. "You must take more care. Just because you cannot die does not mean you can't be harmed."

Don't you think I know that, he wanted to shout. Instead, he asked, "Are they all d-dead?"

His stranger's frown deepened. "Of course not. Merely asleep."

Distantly, Hugh remembered his cell mates in France, snoring peacefully while the Grim Reaper and his stranger haggled over a wager. He looked around at the ruin of his life.

"I'll have to run," he whispered.

To his utter surprise, the stranger stepped forward, closing the distance between them, and reached a hand down. Hugh took it, his own still shaking, and let his elegant, unruffled savior pull him to his feet — seemingly without effort.

The stranger's skin was dry and smooth, untouched by the calluses of hard labor. "Do you not reinvent yourself regularly?" he asked, as though perplexed by Hugh's distress.

"Not regularly enough," Hugh managed.

Would the townsfolk sleep for minutes? Hours? Forever? He couldn't bring himself to ask. He slid his hand free of the stranger's cool grip — missing the support immediately — and went to dig spare clothing out of the ruins of his storage trunk. Keeping his back turned, he pulled it on clumsily, still feeling as though his legs might give out again at any moment.

"And do you still wish to live, Hugh de Ferrers?" asked the velvet voice, without judgement. "Even now?"

Hugh swallowed painfully. "Yes," he said, grabbing a sack from the corner and picturing what he would need to take with him when he fled. "Even now."

Money. Food. Another change of clothing. The bare minimum of his tools necessary for farrier work. A few of his most precious books. He would do what he should have done before — get on a ship, sail to the New World.

The stranger regarded him, his dark expression smoothing. "Then I will see you in another hundred years." One sharply canted eyebrow twitched upward, and a dry note crept into his voice as he added cryptically, "If not before."

Hugh held that unearthly blue gaze for a long moment, the empty sack hanging limp in his hand. He had been a fool, and he'd nearly paid for it in a way that might have driven even an immortal man insane.

"A hundred years," he echoed. "If not before."

NINE

1721 A.D.

NEARLY A CENTURY later, Morpheus stared in bemusement as the dream consciousness of Hugh de Ferrers once again defiled a naked dream image of… well… *him*. This was not precisely a *regular* occurrence, but it had played out enough times over the past two centuries that whichever long-suffering oneiros ended up playing the role of Morpheus immediately came to the throne room and reported it to him.

They probably assumed he took personal control of these particular dreams so that he could direct de Ferrers' unconscious mind down some different path. Indeed, doing so would have been both the obvious and the simplest choice.

The oneiri were forbidden from controlling dreamers' minds. They could not force a particular dream or nightmare on an unwilling participant—a fact which rankled among a certain subset of the creatures. Their function was to focus the dreamer's vision, exploring whatever flotsam and jetsam rose to the surface. Without them, those countless dreaming minds would succumb to the natural randomness of the collective unconscious, turning their nighttime imaginings into so much useless gibberish.

Only Morpheus had the power to cut a dream short or transform it into something unrelated. He could be using that power right now, as de Ferrers swallowed his doppelganger's cock to the root, moaning as though it was the only meal he'd eaten in days. Not for the first time, Morpheus felt his point of view shift, a deep, drawing sensation pulling somewhere inside him.

No. That wasn't right. He should —

The near-silent flutter of familiar wings jerked him back to his *fully clothed* position in the shadowed corner of the spectacular bedroom de Ferrers' mind had conjured. The space next to him twisted, and Iridaceae stood at his shoulder in humanoid form. She tilted her head, birdlike as ever, watching the increasingly fraught scene with the same attention she would give a mouse or a snake before swooping down on it.

"Is that hygienic?" she asked after a long, awkward pause.

Morpheus felt a moment's irrational frustration at the interruption. He directed the emotion outward, swiping a hand across the scene and sending the human back to wakefulness. The dream collapsed into mist, which coalesced into the familiar mirror-covered walls of the throne room.

"You have news?" he asked, pointedly ignoring his familiar's question.

She shook herself as though settling invisible feathers. "Yes. The rumors are true. Your brother hasn't been seen in the Night Lands for months."

Morpheus scowled. Policing his siblings' comings and goings was not his responsibility. A strong argument could be made that it was also not his business, since he would certainly take exception to his family tracking his own movements between the realms.

But… this was Phobetor. His brother, the embodiment of living things' fear.

And… de Ferrers' exuberance aside, Morpheus' domain had suffered a spreading cancer of fear, of late. Perhaps he hadn't always taken such an interest in humanity's foibles, but his visit to the Sublunary during the years of famine in the thirteen hundreds had given him fresh insight into the connection between the humans' dreams and their waking lives.

Interfering with the progression of famine, or plague, or war was neither within his purview, nor within his power. However, the fact that the current wave of fear-driven nightmares coincided with his brother's extended absence was… *concerning*.

"I see," he said. "Perhaps a visit to the Sublunary is in order."

Iridaceae perked up. "You are due to visit your pet human soon, are you not?" She jerked her chin toward the mirrors filled with ever-changing images. "The one who dreams about what you look like beneath your robes."

Patience, he reminded himself, and swallowed the urge to snap at her in irritation.

"He is not mine, nor is he a *pet*. And yes, that excuse will do nicely." He paused, not above a bit of petty revenge. "You shall accompany me."

Her spine straightened in excitement.

"As a human," he finished.

Her jaw dropped. "You expect me to wear *clothes*?" Outrage colored the words, which were delivered in roughly the same tone as a human who'd just been asked to walk over hot coals.

He raised an eyebrow. "That would seem to be the wisest course, yes."

"*Hmph.*" She fluttered again, returning to her owl form and flapping off in a huff.

"Be ready at noonday on the appointed date," he called after her, satisfied that she would now have other things on her mind besides the dreamscene she'd unexpectedly walked in on.

When her graceful avian form disappeared through the archways leading deeper into the palace, he lowered himself onto his throne and leaned his chin thoughtfully on one hand, letting his attention sink into the countless shifting images reflected in the mirrors. Perhaps more clues could be gained from the rushing river of humanity's collective unconscious.

———◆———

When Easter Sunday of 1721 A.D. rolled around a few days later, all he'd gleaned was that the malaise was centered across several different continents, and that it affected humans of many different walks of life.

Iridaceae flounced into the throne room in a high temper, clad in the pastel peacock finery favored by the humans in Hugh de Ferrers' part of the world. Her dark hair had been tamed into tiny ringlets, topped with a lace cap and framed with muslin lappets. The capacious skirts of her *robe volante* draped over a panier formed of hoops so wide that it was almost comical, dwarfing her tiny waist in its boned corset.

She gestured down at the ensemble, color high on her cheeks. "How am I supposed to run or fight in this? Or *hunt*?"

"As to the first and the second," Morpheus said coolly, "you aren't. Though I suspect some humans still manage the third."

Iridaceae sniffed, clearly unconvinced.

His own attire was noticeably less ridiculous, though still ostentatious in a way he disliked. The skirts of his embroidered black silk coat were heavy and pleated, reaching almost to his knees, while the black breeches and white stockings left little to the imagination.

Picking up the thread leading to Hugh de Ferrers, he stepped through the veil separating the Night Lands from the Sublunary, drawing Iridaceae along with him.

London, England was a recognizable landmark even to one who saw it mostly through the dreams of others. The dome of St. Paul's cathedral rose among the skyline, distinctive and unmissable. They were standing outside a respectable-looking townhouse situated along a busy street. The silken thread connected to de Ferrers led inside. All appeared calm, unlike several of the other Easters on which Morpheus had visited the man.

Rather than appear directly at his side, Morpheus raised a hand to the heavy door and grasped the knocker. It echoed dully as he rapped it against the wood. A moment later, it opened, revealing a dour man clad in servant's livery. He eyed them up and down, silently judging, and Morpheus allowed himself a spark of amusement at the idea that a house steward might find a god and his shape-shifting familiar wanting.

"May I help you, sir?" the man asked eventually.

Morpheus found it mildly diverting to play at this game, as though he were not here on important business quite aside from his usual centenary visit.

"We are here to see your master," he said, unsure whether that was in fact de Ferrers' role in this house. He might as easily be a guest, or even another servant. Still, it would be simple enough to determine once they gained entry.

"Very well, sir," said the steward. "I will present him with your card." He held out a gloved hand, expectant.

"That will not be necessary," Morpheus said, abruptly tiring of the game. "He is expecting us."

The man's brow furrowed. "I see, sir. Mister Ferrero is, in fact, expecting company today—but I was led to believe he was anticipating one guest, not two. If you will excuse me for a moment—"

"It's all right, Williams," came a familiar voice. A moment later, de Ferrers appeared in the entryway, a rueful smile twitching at one corner of his lips. "Come in, both of you. Hello, old stranger. And please do introduce me to your charming friend."

◆

A few minutes later, they were installed in a pleasant sitting room with a pot of chocolate and a tray of small cakes before them. De Ferrers sat down across from them, cradling a cup and saucer in his broad hands.

"Iridaceae," he mused. "That's a lovely name. Very classical."

Iridaceae, who had been peering suspiciously at the rich brown liquid in her cup, looked up. "Is it?" she asked. She tilted her head, examining him. "Your hair is white. Aren't you supposed to be immortal? Are you trying to look old?"

De Ferrers blinked, and then huffed out a startled laugh. "You mean the wig? No, this is just what people wear these days. Horrid things, really. They itch, and the powder gets *everywhere*. I take it you're… erm, not from around here?"

Morpheus shot him an unimpressed look. "I daresay you know the answer to that question." He indicated the room, and the house that contained it. "It appears your fortunes are somewhat improved from the last time we met."

The human's expression turned wry. "Well, sometimes there's really no direction to go except up. But yes, I can't complain. Especially given, well, *everything*."

"Everything?" Morpheus echoed.

De Ferrers gave a small shrug. "I'm doing well. Lots of people aren't."

"Indeed." Morpheus set his cup and saucer aside, its contents untouched. "Perhaps you could tell me about that."

Their host sighed. "Let me guess. This is another case like you not knowing about a famine that had been raging for years?"

Morpheus quirked an eyebrow and did not reply. Iridaceae cautiously took a sip of her chocolate, her dark-eyed gaze flicking back and forth between them.

"Right." De Ferrers gazed ceilingward for a moment, as though for strength. "Well, there's the small matter of the economy of Britain and half of Western Europe having collapsed, not to mention the public revelation that we've been engaged as a nation in a slave trade of unimaginable cruelty that spans continents." He set his cup down with a decisive clink, and his tone lightened, almost mockingly. "So, how've you been keeping lately?"

Again, Morpheus ignored the question, along with the disapproval implied in it. "I see." He regarded the human he'd been visiting for five hundred years, assessing the rough body of a medieval blacksmith wrapped in a rich man's finery. "As it happens, my visit today is not merely to ask you if you still wish to continue your long life. I have a task for you."

De Ferrers' eyebrows shot up in surprise. "Oh, you do, do you?" He leaned back on the floral-patterned davenport, crossing his arms. "Well, *that's* hardly ominous at all, now, is it?"

TEN

1721 A.D.

THREE DAYS LATER, Hugh's coach rattled along the cobbles of Lombard Street, bearing him toward Garraway's Coffee House—a shop and meeting place which lay nestled in the shadows of Exchange Alley.

Because apparently, he was an idiot.

Though, perhaps that was unfair. He owed his long existence to his mysterious visitor—and more recently, rescue from some rather dire circumstances indeed. Over the centuries, Hugh had taken wounds that would have killed mortal men, but he had no desire at all to discover what it felt like to wake up after being hanged, drowned, or burned at the stake as a witch.

And so, he had accepted the stranger's request to act on his behalf. In the seat across from him sat Iridaceae, now disguised as a young man, and looking no more thrilled by this turn of events than she had while sitting in his parlor wearing an expensive frock.

She fussed with the sleeves of her embroidered coat, picking at the neat stitches with tiny, pecking movements of her fingernails. At first, Hugh had attempted to make conversation, but it had gone... *awkwardly*. He'd defaulted shortly thereafter to matters of practicality.

"We'll call you Irwin, if that's all right. You can be my nephew, visiting from the continent. I supposedly have an Italian grandfather this time around—hence the last name Ferrero—so it's plausible enough. You're accompanying me to learn the basics of stock trading."

Iridaceae scowled. "Why are females not allowed in this coffee place?"

Hugh hadn't really thought about it before. "I'm not entirely sure, to be honest. I suppose interest in matters of finance isn't considered a ladylike pursuit. At least, that seems to be the reason given for most such things."

"Well, *that's* stupid," said his companion.

Somehow, Hugh didn't think that beginning an explanation of the way a woman's property passed to her husband upon marriage would greatly improve the situation, so he kept silent on the matter. Instead, he returned to the more immediate subject at hand.

"Is there nothing else you can tell me about our purpose here today? Ideally, I'd like to have more knowledge about what I'm walking into."

It's possible that an individual of my acquaintance is meddling where he should not, the stranger had said. *I have located him here in London, but as my direct interference in the matter would be unwise, I require you to look into it on my behalf. Do not attempt to act on your own. Watch, listen, and report to me what you see and hear.*

It was not, to put it mildly, the most forthcoming explanation Hugh had ever heard. Iridaceae merely shrugged.

"Family trouble," she said, and refused to be drawn further.

What Hugh knew of Garraway's Coffee House was this — traders and stockjobbers gathered there to conduct business and discuss news, and the proprietor had an indefensible enthusiasm for a disgusting foreign swill called *tea*, which looked like bilgewater and tasted like stewed twigs.

Hugh wasn't a stupid man. He could see the outline of the sketch taking shape — although the 'family' aspect was an interesting wrinkle. International financial collapse, stock-trading house. That didn't mean he was necessarily the most useful individual, under the circumstances. It was true he'd made his current small fortune mostly on the back of stocks, but after his initial lucky venture, he'd paid someone who actually knew what the blazes he was doing to make investments on his behalf.

That decision had paid him a handsome return in recent years, most notably since the South Sea Company's shocking collapse. Fortunately, Hugh did at least know enough to ensure that he wasn't getting swindled, so he was familiar with the basics of what was being done with his money. He wouldn't look like a complete fool if asked to discuss instruments of finance.

The coach rolled to a halt, depositing them at the door of the coffee house. "Return for us at four p.m., please," Hugh called up to his driver.

Jordan touched the brim of his hat in acknowledgement and whipped up the horses, rejoining the late-morning flow of traffic.

Hugh gave Iridaceae's sullen form a final onceover. She was convincing enough as a lad, with her hard eyes and short ringlets of hair, but —

"Erm, it might be for the best if you left most of the talking to me."

"I have no interest in talking to humans," she said dismissively.

"Then I suppose that works out well." He opened the door for her, following her into the airy, bustling space.

Heavy tables and benches hugged the edges of the long, rectangular room, lit cheerily by a wall of windows looking onto the street. It should have been a warm and welcoming space, but the sour smell of fear choked the atmosphere. It was a scent Hugh associated with battlefields and back alleys, not coffee shops. Beside him, Iridaceae gave a small shudder.

He realized that both of them had stopped dead in their tracks, as though they'd hit a solid wall. Shaking himself free of the odd paralysis, he placed a hand between Iridaceae's slim shoulder blades and urged her toward the nearest free table.

The shop was crowded but not packed. Conversation swirled among groups that broke apart and reformed seemingly at random, rising and falling in pitch. It appeared normal enough on the surface, but a closer look revealed sweaty foreheads and the red-rimmed, bloodshot eyes of men who weren't sleeping well, if at all.

A harried serving-boy approached the table. "Get you something to drink, gents? Coffee and ginger cake? Or, the proprietor just received a shipment of the new black tea, sirs. Far superior to the old green tea, it is."

"Coffee will be fine," Hugh told him firmly. "Cream, no sugar, please."

"I want tea," Iridaceae said. "And cake."

Hugh considered trying to warn her off for about half a second before shrugging and handing the boy a shilling.

"Have you had tea before?" he asked once the server left.

"People dream about it sometimes," she replied defensively, which wasn't terribly illuminating. She'd been dressed in fine clothing when she and his stranger arrived at his townhouse on Easter Sunday. Surely if she harbored dreams of tea and ginger cake, she could have indulged them long before this.

He let it go. "You'll have to tell me if it lives up to your expectations."

Settling back with a determinedly casual air, Hugh tried to ignore the tense atmosphere of the crowd in favor of untangling its ebb and flow. Anywhere people gathered, there were patterns. You only had to look for them—and he'd been observing such patterns far longer than most.

As one would expect when stock traders gathered in numbers, business was being transacted. Paper and money changed hands. Here, too, there was an air that seemed almost frantic.

He turned his attention to those who were more involved in conversation than transaction. Here, the pattern became more obvious. A rather striking gentleman was holding court at the far end of the room, surrounded by a gaggle of onlookers who appeared to be hanging on his every word. When Hugh attempted to focus on the man's face, a shiver went down his spine that felt oddly like dread.

"Over there," he murmured, flicking his chin in the man's direction.

Iridaceae followed his gaze with limited interest. "Yes, that's him. Isn't it obvious?"

"It might have been obvious a bit sooner if you'd said something," Hugh pointed out, trying not to let his irrational frisson of fear bleed into frustration with her oddness.

She opened her mouth to reply, only to be distracted by the arrival of their order. As she fell on the cake like a starving wolf, Hugh held up a hand to prevent the server from scurrying off.

"Who is that man?" he asked, indicating their target. When the boy hesitated, Hugh dug a farthing out of his pocket and passed it over.

It disappeared in a flash. "You mean Mister Timor? Over from South America, he is. Comes in here most days, talkin' about the South Sea Company. Guess he's a… what do you call it? An *insider*."

"I see," Hugh told him. "Thank you."

Iridaceae was sipping her tea, a look of intense concentration on her face as she set it down. "This is good," she said.

The boy smiled. "Better with milk and sugar, if you ask me."

Iridaceae raised an eyebrow and immediately started dumping sugar cubes into her cup.

"I'd like to get closer," Hugh said. "I want to hear what he's saying. Let's move tables."

The cake plate had already been reduced to a few forlorn crumbs, but Iridaceae poured milk into her teacup and clutched it to her chest like a treas-ure. Hugh picked up his untouched coffee and led the way to the fringes of the gathered group.

"I've had word from Parliament that their in-vestigation into the conduct of the Chancellor of the Exchequer has revealed *widespread* corruption," the man was saying, in a voice like wind rustling through the branches of dead trees. "There are whis-pers that the scandal may rise to the very throne itself."

Excited muttering swept through the little as-semblage. Several people broke away, hurrying toward the groups engaged in trading stock shares.

"We all knew that the Chancellor had been tak-ing bribes from the South Sea Company's board of directors!" someone called.

"And Parliament, too!" said someone else. "It's the only reason their stock rose so high in the first place! Without Parliament's ridiculous new laws, none of this would have happened!"

"And they're the ones investigating it now?" another person demanded. "How does that make any sense?"

More unhappy murmurs swelled and ebbed.

The man at the center of the crowd smiled a thin smile. "Ah, well. It's all unraveling now. I daresay before long, the South Sea Company's stock won't be worth the paper it's printed on."

Several more people hurried off, presumably to sell their shares for whatever they could get. And just like that, Hugh knew exactly what was happen-ing here. Like a lady's hat blowing across a busy street, spooking one carriage horse — which then went on to spook others until the entire street descended into chaos—the man with the thin smile and the stormy green eyes was stoking fear in his listeners, driving them to rash action that would ultimately harm them.

"Now just a minute," Hugh said, rising to his feet. "That stock may not be worth the outrageous amount people were paying for it a year ago, but it's worth something. I should know—my financial agent has made me a small fortune short-selling it since last August."

It was perfectly true. Richard Winston-Smythe had a sour face and a keen eye for stocks. He'd convinced Hugh to borrow shares when the price had been near a thousand pounds. Then he'd immediately sold them at that ridiculously inflated price, only to buy them back later for a fraction of the cost, just in time to return the borrowed shares to the lender. Smythe had recently declared the carnage largely complete, with the share price now hovering around one hundred pounds—down over ninety percent.

Hugh lifted his chin. "I'll wager Mister Timor here is engaged in the same game I was, only he's trying to help things along by sowing panic. Have you actually looked at the company's financials, or are you all just following along blindly, like a bunch of sheep being driven toward the edge of a cliff?"

The conversation around him went silent. All eyes turned to Timor, this time with suspicion instead of fear. Timor's green gaze, by contrast, was only for Hugh—and Hugh felt a freezing sense of foreboding grip his throat and lungs beneath the power of that cold stare.

ELEVEN

1721 A.D.

A SMALL HAND gripped Hugh's elbow. "*We need to leave,*" Iridaceae hissed in his ear, tugging at him with fingers that suddenly felt like talons digging into his skin.

The spark of pain shocked Hugh free of his immobility, even if he still felt like a rabbit hypnotized by the eyes of a snake. Too late, he remembered the stranger's admonition—*do not attempt to act on your own.* An instant later, it occurred to him to be concerned about the family of a man who also called the Grim Reaper a companion.

"Er, yes," he said. "Perhaps that would be for the best."

He let Iridaceae pull him toward the door. Around them, stock traders muttered unhappily, no doubt less than impressed by his blithe boasting of making a fortune on the backs of their collective panic. The glares and imprecations of the other patrons were little more than buzzing gnats as far as Hugh was concerned. It was Timor's cold gaze that made the back of his neck prickle with the sixth sense of unknown danger.

The sensation didn't abate until the door of the coffee house swung closed behind them, its bell tinkling merrily. Only then did the tense knot between Hugh's shoulder blades loosen, as though someone who'd been standing behind him with a knife, poised to strike, had changed their mind and lowered it.

"Stupid human!" Iridaceae snapped, looking around at the brisk midday cart- and foot-traffic filling Exchange Alley. "Quickly, how do we get your silly coach-thing back here?"

"We don't," Hugh said blankly. Did she expect him to produce a carrier pigeon from his coat pockets?

"Well, where is it?" she demanded. "Can we take one of these instead?" She gestured at the drovers' carts and other random conveyances traversing the narrow alley.

"No, we can't," Hugh said, with as firm a tone as he could manage. "Knowing Jordan, he's probably parked the carriage at Moorfields. We could walk in that direction—though it might make more sense to wait across the road from Garraway's, so we don't miss him."

"No, it really wouldn't," Iridaceae said. "Walk. *Now*."

She tugged his arm again, but she was heading in the wrong direction for Moorfields—back toward Lombard Street.

"Fine," he said, still queasy with unaccustomed disquiet. "But it's this way."

He pointed to where the warren of Exchange Alley split at a right angle, with the north branch narrowing to a point that only accommodated foot traffic. It emerged onto Cornhill Road, he knew. From there, they'd be able to walk up Moorgate and search for Jordan, who was doubtless whiling away the hours until he was needed again with a pint of beer and a meat pie from one of the open-air stalls in the area.

Iridaceae gave the claustrophobic covered alley a look of deep misgivings, but she followed Hugh as he strode into the shadowed dimness.

Hugh wasn't a fool. He had a cosh secreted in his coat, along with far too many years' experience in fighting off ruffians who mistakenly assumed him an easy mark. Nevertheless, he'd barely led the way beneath the overhanging building that covered this fork of the tunnel-like alley when the feeling of danger poised inches from his back returned. The sudden chill of it stole his breath, and he couldn't help whirling to look over his shoulder.

There was nothing there.

"Come *on*," Iridaceae said through gritted teeth.

Hugh turned to continue walking, aware of the ridiculous, staccato rhythm of his heartbeat. He felt like a child jumping at shadows—and he hadn't been a child in more than five hundred years.

A figure stepped in front of them, blocking their progress. The person seemed to have materialized from nothing. There were no doorways nearby, no nooks or crannies between buildings where the unnaturally tall, thin silhouette could have concealed itself. The now familiar prickling fear drenched Hugh anew, like a bucket of dank, chilly water.

Iridaceae made a wordless sound halfway between irritation and alarm. She grabbed Hugh's hand and darted back the way they'd come, but now the same tall, thin figure was blocking that direction as well.

Hugh's vision wavered as his mind attempted to untangle the impossibility of the man being in two places at once. He tried to crane his head around, but he couldn't seem to get both of the figures in his field of vision at once. The feeling of animal panic was pressing in from all sides, and without knowing how he ended up there, he found his back thumping against the damp stone of the alley wall.

Abruptly, there was only one figure. It loomed in front of him, gazing down its beaky nose with eyes that seemed to glow from within—a sickly green light. Beside him, Iridaceae, too, had backed against the wall.

The man tilted his head, considering. "Hugh de Ferrers," he said, in the familiar voice like wind through dry leaves. "Or perhaps I should say, Hugh Ferrero. You are meddling in things you should have left well alone."

His eyes flickered over Iridaceae. She stiffened at Hugh's side. His gaze narrowed, and he returned it to Hugh, pinning him in place as effectively as a hand on the chest.

"What is your connection with *this creature*?" he spat.

Iridaceae let out an offended squawk, but the man only scoffed. "Quiet, mongrel—unless you want your wings clipped."

In the next instant, Iridaceae broke free of whatever strange force held them paralyzed. But instead of running, she lifted her arms, and the air around her twisted. An owl flapped upward in a flurry of brown feathers, its wings slapping the air inches from their assailant's face.

The man didn't even flinch—not that Hugh retained enough command of his own senses to take advantage of the distraction. He was having difficulty breathing, not helped by the sudden concern that he'd somehow hallucinated a girl turning into a bird and flying away.

Hugh's tormenter let out a soft grunt of irritation before appearing to dismiss Iridaceae's escape… if that part had, in fact, been real.

"I ask again," said the man, in the tone of someone not accustomed to repeating himself. "What is your connection to my brother's familiar? For that matter, what is your connection *to my brother?*"

Hugh's mouth opened and closed a couple of times. "I-I don't know what you mean," he stammered, even though he could hazard a reasonable guess.

Family trouble, Iridaceae had said.

"Oh, I think you do," the man practically purred. He lifted a hand, tilting Hugh's face up with a single finger pressed under his chin.

Hugh's skin crawled. The long-buried memory of the Grim Reaper with his dark robes and cruel eyes rose unbidden. But this was different than the instinctual animal terror and rage that had flooded his mind whenever he was in the presence of the embodiment of death. That had been the gut-deep awareness of a deer pierced by a hunter's arrow, or a lamb meeting the gaze of its slaughterer.

This was something else—the creeping horror at the inevitability of grief and betrayal. The knowledge that your worst fear lurked just beyond the edge of your peripheral vision, waiting to pounce.

The man's finger and thumb squeezed, trapping Hugh's chin and holding him in place.

"I could twist your mind into madness with a single thought." He sounded wistful, as though he could think of no more pleasant way to pass an afternoon. His thumb caressed Hugh's skin, and it felt like spider legs crawling over him.

Hugh shuddered.

He opened his mouth, struggling to draw breath for speech — to disavow any knowledge once again? To spill everything he knew about his stranger? He wasn't certain. Surely a man could not survive for long with his heart pounding as fast and thready as his seemed to be.

A second shadow loomed over Hugh in the cramped alley.

"*Enough.*" The band around his chest snapped, and he gasped in air as the welcome voice of his stranger echoed against the stone walls. Hugh's assailant did not release the light grip he still held on Hugh's chin, but he did turn his head slowly toward its source. Hugh rolled his eyes, desperate for the sight of his stranger's pale, hawklike face.

The stranger stood, chin up and jaw set, with a very familiar owl perched on his shoulder. It was not, Hugh realized, the first time he had seen him thus. The owl had accompanied him in 1521 as well, soaring down from the nearby trees to settle on its master's shoulder.

His mind struggled to connect the bird with the odd girl he'd come to know as Iridaceae, but the conclusion was inescapable. More magic. More impossible sorcery. More proof, if any were needed, that the townsfolk of Ipswich had been onto something when they'd showed up at Hugh's door to accuse him of witchcraft and consorting with de-mons.

"*Brother*." Hugh's tormenter caressed the word like a lover, drawing it out. "What an unexpected... *pleasure*." The final word dripped irony like fresh blood from a dagger.

"Release the human." His stranger's words were ice—a frozen lake with terrifying monsters writhing beneath the surface. Darkness crept out-ward from his eyes like a living thing seeking release.

But the fingers trapping Hugh in place didn't so much as waver. His tormenter studied Hugh with, if anything, more interest than before.

"Oh, dear," he said. "Are you keeping pets again, little brother? Could it be that you thought to spy on me with these puny creatures?"

The owl let out an offended warble and flut-tered its wings.

Hugh's stranger didn't rise to the bait. "You are meddling in the Sublunary, *brother*. Overstepping your bounds in an attempt to... what? Gain more power? Feed your endless addiction?"

The stranger's brother hissed angrily, his fin-gers twitching against Hugh's flesh. "What you call '*bounds*,' I call *bondage*. Why should we submit our-selves to such nonsense when we are so far above them?" He turned a thin, ugly smile on Hugh, who felt his gut roil unpleasantly. "Why should we not meddle in the Sublunary, when they are so *very*... *easy*... to *frighten*?"

With each word, the grip on Hugh's chin tightened. Hugh's breathing went ragged, his vision swimming as red-gray mist swirled at the edges.

"This man is under my protection," said Hugh's stranger. "And since I suspect that declaration will hold no weight with you, you should know that he is also under *Thanatus'* protection."

The fingers trapping him wavered. "Thanatus? What business has he with such a creature?"

"Perhaps you will return to your own realm and ask him yourself," said Hugh's stranger, without inflection.

A tendon worked in his assailant's jaw. Hugh watched it jump and twitch with terrified fascination.

"Perhaps *you* will return to *your* own realm and go fuck yourself, little brother." Finally — *finally* — the fingers released him. Hugh's knees chose that moment to turn to pudding, and he slid down the grimy wall. His tormenter sneered at him. "Or perhaps you would prefer to sodomize one of your toys instead. Whatever the case, stay out of my affairs, or suffer the consequences."

The owl squawked again, and the noise truly did remind Hugh of Iridaceae in full outrage. Before the echoes faded, Hugh's tormenter had disappeared as mysteriously as he'd come — there one moment and gone the next.

Hugh scrubbed a shaking hand down his face. "What," he began plaintively, "the ever-bleedin' *fuck* was *that* about?"

TWELVE

1721 A.D.

MORPHEUS STARED DOWN at the human he'd placed in harm's way, debating the best course of action. What had seemed at the time like an obvious solution to the conundrum of dealing with his brother, now felt like the worst kind of folly.

"Can you stand?" he asked, since the answer was not a foregone conclusion after such concentrated attention from Phobetor, the embodiment of fear. He ignored de Ferrers' plaintive question about what was going on, since the answer would take longer than he cared to spend standing in a stinking alley.

"Of course, I can stand," de Ferrers snapped. "You secretive, *infuriating*—"

The human scrabbled behind him for purchase against the wall, using it to lever himself to his feet. He'd made it about halfway up when the blood drained abruptly from his face, his eyes rolled back in his head, and he fainted dead away.

Iridaceae flapped down from Morpheus' shoulder, shifting into human form beside him. She regarded the crumpled figure against the wall with her head tilted to one side.

Silence stretched.

"We could just leave him here," she said hopefully.

"We are *not* leaving him here." Morpheus kept his tone firm. He looked around at their thoroughly uninspiring surroundings, unwilling to admit how little familiarity he had with the day-to-day workings of the Sublunary in these modern times.

Iridaceae let out a put-upon sigh. "He said something about his carriage thingy returning to the coffee shop for us at four p.m."

No sunlight penetrated the covered alleyway, but Morpheus knew it was slightly past midday in this part of the world. The wait would be several hours, and he could not be entirely certain Phobetor wouldn't return to continue his fearmongering inside Garraway's coffee house. Returning there would be too dangerous now that de Ferrers had attracted the attention of the God of Fear.

"Carrying him back to Garraway's isn't an option," he decided. Indeed, they were getting a number of strange looks from the thin trickle of passersby. A few even turned and retreated the way they'd come, rather than risk getting involved in whatever was happening. Apparently, two strange people leaning over an unconscious, well-dressed man in a dark alley was cause for some concern among London's citizens.

Iridaceae's sigh was louder this time. "He also said the carriage was parked somewhere called Moorfields, and it was in that direction." She pointed.

Perhaps that would be a better option. "Could you recognize the carriage from the air?" he asked.

She shrugged. "Probably."

"Very well. Fly to this *Moorfields* place and find it. Inform the driver where to find us and return with him as quickly as you can." He gave Iridaceae a severe look. "Be discreet."

"I'm always discreet!" she said, and immediately shifted into owl form without bothering to check the alley for human witnesses.

Fortunately, there weren't any. Morpheus released a slow breath through his nose and crouched in front of de Ferrers. One thing about it — at least the shock of his brother's power wouldn't kill the man. Not permanently, at least.

———◆———

It was some considerable time later when a lad in red livery came hurrying down the alley at Iridaceae's heels. Morpheus was somewhat relieved by the fact that she was in human form, and still wearing appropriate clothing.

"What's wrong with him, sir?" the driver asked breathlessly, gaping at his unconscious employer.

The wait, while tiresome, had given Morpheus ample time to concoct a plausible story. "He was set upon by an assailant. His attacker ran away, but not before dealing him a blow to the head."

The driver paled. "Oh, dear. Head injuries can be serious. Quickly, sir, let's get him in the carriage and back to his house. If he hasn't woken up by then, I'll go and find a doctor for him."

Morpheus allowed the lad to help him carry de Ferrers to the end of the alley and bundle him into the waiting carriage. The driver flipped a coin to the small boy holding the horses, and the child immediately scampered off. He climbed into the seat at the front of the conveyance, taking up the reins. With a flick of the whip, they were moving.

The vehicle clattered over the cobblestone roads, jouncing and jarring them unpleasantly. They'd been underway for only a few minutes when de Ferrers jerked awake with a gasp, like a man surfacing from drowning.

"All is well," Morpheus told him, which was probably an exaggeration.

"Your carriage looks very much like all the other carriages from the air," Iridaceae said. "You might consider having it painted puce, so it would be more distinctive. Or perhaps chartreuse if you prefer it."

De Ferrers blinked at them. "Wh-what?"

Morpheus frowned. "I told you to observe, not to act. Yet you managed to attract my brother's attention, and now all of us will reap the consequences."

Visibly recalling himself to the waking world and what had occurred therein, de Ferrers straightened in the lavishly upholstered seat. "Oh. The coffee house. Right." He turned bleary eyes on Iridaceae. "Are you all right? Both of you?"

"He threatened to cut my wings off!" Iridaceae said. "I should have pecked his eyes out!"

"Somehow I doubt that would have improved the situation." Morpheus returned his attention to the human across from him. "Your driver believes you were accosted by a criminal in the alley and suffered a blow to the head. No doubt he will be relieved that you are awake."

De Ferrers' gaze narrowed. "Instead, I was accosted by... *your brother*. Who is apparently fanning the flames of a stock market panic that has decimated England's economy over the course of the last year. And who—like you and your jolly friend the Grim Reaper—clearly isn't human." He paused. "Oh, and lest I forget, Iridaceae *is an owl*. Unless I hallucinated that part."

Iridaceae preened. Morpheus did not reply.

De Ferrers made an incoherent noise of frustration. "In case it wasn't obvious, this is the part where you explain what in blazes is going on! Who are you? Who—or what— is your brother? Mister *Timor*? I did actually take the time to learn Latin late in the last century, by the way."

"That is not his name," Morpheus said. He didn't add that it might as well have been. Timor was one of several Latin words for fear.

The human threw up his hands in frustration. "Fine. Then what *is* his name? For that matter, what is *your* name?"

Morpheus held his gaze unflinchingly. "The answers to your questions would only put you in more danger. Avoid my brother's notice, and I have no doubt he will forget about you entirely before long. Embroil yourself further in my affairs, and I may not be able to protect you from the consequences."

De Ferrers' expression went icy. "I see. So, once again, I am of use to you when you wish me to be, but not worthy of enough consideration to know who it is that uses me in such a way. To you, I am but a pair of dice thrown—and later forgotten—in the depths of a gambling hell."

Morpheus knew his own expression had grown equally cold. "Live your life, Hugh de Ferrers. Do not concern yourself with events outside your ken.

We will meet again in one hundred years. Until then, I wish you to be safe. This was a mistake."

Without further ceremony, he gathered Iridaceae inside his aura and swept them both into the liminal space between realms—returning to the Night Lands with de Ferrers' cry of, "No, wait!" echoing in his ears.

THIRTEEN

1821 A.D.

ON EASTER SUNDAY of 1821, Morpheus appeared in the midst of a raucous, chanting crowd. At his approach, Hugh de Ferrers glanced up, raising an eyebrow at him.

"Ah. Hello there, *Morpheus*," he said sharply, his voice just loud enough to be heard over the surrounding noise. "Welcome to Edinburgh. Happy Easter. Sorry about the riots."

Morpheus paused, momentarily arrested. To hear his name on the human's lips was unexpected, to put it mildly — but perhaps it shouldn't have been. He stepped forward to join the human and lifted his own eyebrow in rejoinder.

"This seems a rather atypical gathering for Easter Sunday," he replied in kind, ignoring de Ferrers' rather startling sally.

He'd let too much slip during his ill-conceived meeting with the man in 1721. For all that de Ferrers was a medieval peasant at heart, he wasn't a fool. 'Timor' had been a lazy pseudonym for the God of Fear, while the Greeks and Romans had been sticklers when it came to writing down their myths.

As de Ferrers had said at the time, he understood Latin. He'd obviously done his research and made an obvious, if unfortunate, connection. That didn't mean Morpheus had any intention of confirming it.

De Ferrers stared at him for a long moment, as though waiting to see if he would respond further.

When no reaction was forthcoming, he looked briefly heavenward, as if for strength, before replying to Morpheus' implied question about the excited mob.

"This is Cowgate, in Old Town. Well, the edge of it, anyway. It's a very nasty place, full to bursting with a lot of extremely poor people who've decided they're tired of having no money, no jobs, and no political representation."

The human had to raise his voice even higher to be heard over the growing commotion around them, and Morpheus tilted his head curiously as he registered the unfamiliar shape and cadence of the words.

"Your accent is different," he accused.

De Ferrers snorted, slipping into his normal voice. "Yes, well—England got a bit too hot for me after the Peterloo riots. So now I'm Hugh Fergusson; a good Scotsman, born and bred. Regular chameleon, me."

"You have become political?" Morpheus asked skeptically.

Since their last meeting, he'd made a habit to maintain more of an awareness of events in this part of the Sublunary, if only to keep watch for further interference from Phobetor.

The Peterloo Massacre had been an unfortunate incident in the city of Manchester, during which armed and mounted soldiers had ridden down members of a peaceful crowd protesting for political reform in St. Peter's Square. Hundreds had been injured or killed, and journalists had coined the name as a play on the Battle of Waterloo. Morpheus had been unable to determine if Phobetor had been involved, but he couldn't rule it out.

"Political?" de Ferrers echoed. "Am I a *radical*, you mean?" He shrugged, returning to his assumed Scottish accent. "Dunno. If thinking people should have a say in their own destiny—preferably with enough food to eat and a roof over their heads—makes me radical, then maybe so. But mostly, I keep wondering if your brother has anything to do with things like this."

Morpheus frowned. "Did I not warn you to avoid my brother's notice?"

De Ferrers met his gaze flatly, not breaking it even when a group of excited youths shoved past, jostling him. "That was a hundred years ago. I got bored."

Alarm rose in Morpheus' chest, though he could not have said precisely why. "I never took you for a fool, Hugh *Fergusson*."

The human's unimpressed stare didn't waver. "Oh, I think you did, actually." Finally, he blinked, some of the intensity draining away from his demeanor.

He looked around with a wry expression. "Hope this mess doesn't go bad like it did in Manchester. Though I guess if it does, they can call it Easterloo." A sigh. "At least I'm not on the speakers' platform this time," he added.

Morpheus followed his gaze to the crowd encircling them, taking in the chaos. "Perhaps this assembly will be less fraught."

As if his words had been some sort of signal, screams erupted from the far edge of the square.

"*Wonderful.* You just had to go and say something!" said de Ferrers, a few seconds before the crowd heaved, surging away from whatever had alarmed the humans in that direction.

Morpheus had paid little attention to their wider surroundings beyond noticing that they smelled quite bad. Now, he used his advantage of height to scan the area. The buildings behind them were cramped and squalid, leaning against each other like drunkards, while those on the far side appeared markedly nicer, boasting classical architecture and clean, well-maintained facades.

A line of uniformed men on horseback waded into the crowd from that end of the square, even as the mob attempted to flee before them.

"Ah. It appears I was mistaken," he called, as de Ferrers battled to stay upright among the crush of bodies. "You should remove yourself to safety post haste."

Even in their panic, the humans parted around Morpheus like water around a boulder. De Ferrers lunged forward and darted out a hand, grasping his forearm to keep them from becoming separated in the confusion.

"Thanks!" he said, a bit frantically. "I'll get right on that!"

Morpheus stared down at the fingers gripping his dark topcoat, startled by the warmth he could feel seeping through the fabric. The direct contact had the effect of pulling de Ferrers into the small bubble of calm surrounding him. For that reason, he didn't shake off the unexpected touch.

The human tugged him forward... trying to drag him to safety, Morpheus realized. It was utterly unnecessary, of course; though he supposed de Ferrers had no way of knowing that.

Morpheus drew breath to chastise the man for not focusing on his own wellbeing, but the words died in his throat when a massive, concussive *boom!* erupted nearby, sending bodies and debris flying.

It was sheer instinct to slip partway into the space between dimensions before the flying shrapnel reached his physical form. When he slipped back, it was to find de Ferrers lying on the ground several feet away, unmoving. Panicked people stumbled over his body, trampling him without thought in their haste to get away.

Another explosion ripped the air, closer to the advancing riders... followed by a third, and then a fourth. Horses squealed, rearing and twisting away; trying to bolt. Morpheus recognized the destructive effects of gunpowder grenades, a frequent component in the nightmares of soldiers who'd survived the Napoleonic Wars.

De Ferrers was immortal. Whatever injuries he had sustained during the blast, he would recover. And yet... Morpheus felt loath to leave him to the mercy of the panicked mob. Moving against the tide of humanity, he forged a path to his companion's side, his presence opening a small space around the crumpled body — one of several that had succumbed to the first blast.

The human's head was half-gone, his skull shattered and grisly where some chunk of brick or stone had slammed into it. Morpheus stared at the horrific injury in sick fascination, abruptly unsure if he'd somehow been drawn from the waking world back into the realm of the oneiri's nightmares.

He continued to stare, as around him the mounted troops gradually overcame the crowd, forcing it to disperse. The press of people grew less and less, until only a few humans wandered around the square, looking dazed and lost. They picked their way amongst dozens of fallen bodies—some of which were groaning or flopping weakly on the ground.

Morpheus didn't know where in this city de Ferrers might keep rooms; whether he had friends or even a family who might notice his absence. He also knew little of the death rituals in this part of the world. However, he was reasonably certain that there was a wait of one or more days between death and burial.

Given that he had no place in the Sublunary to which he might take de Ferrers' body for safekeeping while he healed—and that carrying a full-grown man by himself would be ridiculously conspicuous, anyway—he resolved to watch over the human from a position of safety in the boundary separating the waking world from the Night Lands.

Slipping sideways into the ether, he settled in to wait.

The troops left; their grisly work done. As the hours passed, a trickle of new people began to arrive in the square, moving from body to body. Taking away the injured, and occasionally collapsing next to an unmoving corpse, wailing or weeping with grief.

No one came for de Ferrers.

It was dusk when the wagons arrived, drawn by powerful horses that snorted and pawed unhappily upon breathing in the scent of death. All of those who still lived were loaded onto the first two wagons, while the unclaimed dead were wrapped in sheets and tossed onto the third like cordwood.

De Ferrers' unconscious mind was a low, monotone hum—barely detectable. Rather than trust his ability to trace it, Morpheus followed the wagon on foot in the waking world, keeping to the shadows at the edges of humanity's awareness.

The wagon wended its way past the classical buildings on the south side of the square, which Morpheus now recognized as an institution of learning—one of the humans' ornate temples to education. A plaque near an arched iron gate read *University of Edinburgh*. Idly, Morpheus wondered at its proximity to an area of such poverty and squalor.

The city beyond was neither as grand as the university, nor as decrepit as the ramshackle, drunken buildings of Cowgate. The wagon stopped in front of a structure that might once have been a chapel, but now held none of the trappings of the humans' new religion.

Men emerged to help unload the bodies, taking them one by one through the arched double doors. When they returned for de Ferrers' sheet-wrapped corpse, Morpheus silently followed them inside. The men trudged down a narrow, poorly lit staircase, to a stone vault where the other bodies lay on the floor in a neat row.

They laid de Ferrers down at the end. Blood seeped through the dingy white of the sheet at his head, staining it rusty.

A rat-faced man with thinning hair moved from corpse to corpse, peeling back the makeshift shrouds to examine them.

"Good, good," he muttered, tutting occasionally when he came to a particularly blood-soaked shroud. When he was finished, he straightened and beckoned to one of the workmen from the wagon. "You. Go find the resurrection men down on Guthrie Street. Let them know I've got a dozen cadavers for sale. Tell them they'd best hurry if they want 'em fresh."

FOURTEEN

1821 A.D.

THE IRONY WASN'T lost on Morpheus, even though he didn't know what a 'resurrection man' might be in this context. Still, based on the name, they'd chosen and apt subject in de Ferrers.

Since Morpheus still had no good place to take the human in the Sublunary, and since selling bodies implied haggling over price and, presumably, transport to a different location, he continued to wait and watch.

Time was on de Ferrers' side. It would be simpler to extract him when he was once more conscious, able to direct Morpheus to his own dwelling or another safe place. In truth, Morpheus was unsure how long such a feat of recovery might take, given the nature and severity of his head injury. With luck, it would not be overly long.

He remained outside the scope of the humans' senses, seeing but unseen. Presently, new footsteps echoed down the stone staircase, and the rat-faced man who'd taken charge of the body roused himself to meet them.

"Hear you've got some warm ones for us?" said one of the newcomers — a gruff man with a wide face and dark muttonchop whiskers. Morpheus stretched out his senses, picking up the threads of the man and his companions. Avarice colored his daydreams, while the others' dreams of coin were tainted with superstition and nervousness.

The rat-faced man nodded eagerly. "Still in rigor mortis—not even twelve hours since they died. See for yourself!"

The gruff man wrinkled his nose. "They reek like two-week-old fish."

Rat-face shrugged. "From Cowgate, aren't they? Can't help it—that's just how people smell down there."

The newcomer sighed. "Let's see 'em, then."

Once again, the ritual of pulling back sheets and examining bodies was repeated, this time in more detail.

"Guess we know where you got 'em from, eh?" said the gruff man, straightening from Hugh at the end of the row.

"It's perfect, though, innit?" rat-face replied. "These were the leftovers. No one came and got them, so that means no one missed 'em enough to come looking. My lads picked 'em up quiet-like, so as far as anyone knows, they were never there at all."

The gruff man grunted. "They're in right poor condition. Look at this one—he's missing half his head!" He gestured sharply at de Ferrers.

"Well, then, I guess you can leave them and go on to the next seller who happens to have a dozen fresh bodies lying around for the anatomists!" Rat-face gestured, equally sharply, and the pair fell to haggling over payment.

This last exchange was at least somewhat enlightening. *Anatomists*, the man had said. Morpheus was aware that there had been increasing interest over the past few centuries regarding accuracy in human art. Perhaps the nearby university had artists and sculptors in need of bodies for study, that they might more correctly portray the details of human form and movement in their works.

Eventually, an agreement of some sort was reached, though rat-face did not appear pleased.

"It's barely worth my while. Not after I pay the men for the wagon and the labor." His voice held a hint of a whine. "Maybe next time I'll do the deal myself, direct-like."

The gruff man handed over a purse that clinked when rat-face took it. "You do that, old chum," he said, sounding supremely unconcerned.

Rat-faced muttered something uncomplimentary, but the purse disappeared inside his shapeless coat quickly enough. The gruff man turned to his companions.

"Get them into the tunnels," he ordered. "I'll go on ahead and have a word with my contact."

Despite some genuine curiosity about this *contact* and the exact nature of the gruff man's grisly business, Morpheus opted to stay with de Ferrers' body rather than follow him. As before, he made use of the shadows and blind spots in the humans' minds to observe without being observed.

The broad-shouldered workmen rewrapped the makeshift shrouds around the bodies and began hauling them through a door at the far end of the vault, poorly secured with a broken metal gate. The door led into a warren of damp underground passages riddled with rats and the detritus of human habitation. They passed low-ceilinged recesses, some housing whole families crammed into the murky darkness.

Wide-eyed urchins with thin, pasty faces peered out at the passing procession of death; their way lit only by the occasional oil lantern hanging on the slimy walls. It was an entire underground city, albeit one without any sort of basic amenities. Morpheus began to understand what de Ferrers had meant about the residents' extreme poverty.

No one questioned the transportation of a dozen bodies through the surreal underworld. Perhaps death was merely that much of a common sight here, or perhaps the gruff man's trade was well known in this area.

They fetched up in a vault much like the one where the rat-faced man had held court before, and which Morpheus estimated to be quite near the university. Again, they waited, until the gruff man returned in the company of a bookish youngster with a nervous demeanor, wearing passably good clothing compared to the workmen's rough garments.

"Bring them through, please," he said, in precise, clipped tones. "There's some ice left over in the storage room after the last delivery."

Unlike the workers, whose daydreams still ran toward money, the bookish youth was lost in thoughts of the appreciation he might garner from a respected authority figure.

"You payin' us now?" asked one of the men carrying de Ferrers.

"Payment is between you and your employer," the youth snapped. "He's already been reimbursed.

And I daresay you'll make a fair penny from selling the clothing and belongings."

That seemed to satisfy the men, who followed him through a final stretch of tunnels, these noticeably better lit than the ones they'd traversed to get here. The room at the end of the corridor had a heavy door with a lock. Chill air spilled out when the lad opened it, distinctly colder than the clammy atmosphere of the underground tunnels.

Inside, half-melted blocks of ice sat atop piles of sawdust. A lone form covered by a shroud lay in one corner, the scent of decay emanating from it like a beacon.

"Lay them down and remove their clothing," the youth ordered. "Every single stitch, mind. Corpses aren't property and therefore can't be stolen, but belongings can. The university mustn't be seen to do anything illegal, after all."

Several of the men muttered epithets, but they did as they were told. Morpheus watched from the unseen shadows as the bodies were summarily stripped to bare skin, a slow roil of anger taking him by surprise.

The humans were dead. They had no further need of their belongings — with the notable exception of de Ferrers. Their souls had already fled to his uncle's domain within the Night Lands. Yet, something about the casual disrespect toward the dead made Morpheus consider abandoning his plan in favor of dragging these men into nightmare-plagued sleep. He could deliver them to the oneiri with a thought, and then spirit de Ferrers' body away to… where, exactly?

He clenched his jaw, setting his irrational anger aside as unhelpful.

Eventually, the men left with their boon of stolen clothing and belongings. The youth extinguished the lamps and left as well; a heavy click from the door signifying the turn of the lock.

Darkness was no deterrent to a son of Nox and Somnus. Nor was the lock… though it would be a deterrent for de Ferrers, should he wake in the night. Morpheus turned inward, but the thread of the man's subconscious remained nothing more than white noise. Stepping fully into the waking world, he crossed to the blood-soaked shroud covering the only human Morpheus had ever viewed as his personal responsibility.

He crouched and pulled the sheet back, seeing the shape of de Ferrers' skull in tones of gray on gray, without the need for light. It was already knitting itself back together, much different from the gruesome gap he had witnessed in the aftermath of the grenade's explosion. It was not, however, healed. Merely improved.

Again, simmering anger at de Ferrers' treatment by these *resurrection men* rose… and again, he pushed it away.

After a long moment's contemplation, Morpheus shrugged his greatcoat from his shoulders and laid it over the naked human, covering him from chest to ankle. In many ways, it was a meaningless gesture. Like all his creations, the coat was only as real as Morpheus willed it to be — the stuff of dreams in the most literal sense. It was also the best he had to offer in these circumstances.

At some point—probably on the morrow—several university students would be in for a shock when they discovered that one of their anatomy subjects was, in fact, still alive. Perhaps de Ferrers would look back on this interlude at their next meeting with wry amusement, holding Morpheus' gaze with a self-deprecating laugh as they recounted the startlement on the students' faces.

Morpheus settled in to wait, trusting in his oneiri to oversee the night's dreams in his absence.

———◆———

The morning brought no light to the underground storage room, but it did bring the faint sound of footsteps echoing from beyond the heavy door.

De Ferrers' wound was now little more than an indentation in his left temple, though there was no change in the untethered hum of his mind. Morpheus whisked his coat away and swung it over his shoulders as the lock clanked open, stepping back into the shadows, both literal and figurative.

"I think they came from the riot yesterday afternoon, Doctor Barclay." The voice of the bookish youth from the previous evening filtered in as the door swung open. "They're a bit banged up, but they should be nice and fresh except for that one left over from last Friday."

Faint light from the corridor streamed in, silhouetting two figures in the doorway. They stepped inside, the slender figure of the youngster flitting around the room to light the lanterns hanging on the walls. The second figure was older—a gray-haired man with a prominent, bulbous nose and bushy eyebrows.

"Very good, McCready," he said in a heavy burr. "I've a lecture in twenty minutes. Have those three brought down to the theater." He indicated de Ferrers and the two sheet-wrapped forms next to him with a careless wave. "Doctors Bell and Monro will doubtless find a use for the others before they're too far gone."

"Yes, sir," replied the youth. "Very good, sir!"

The pair departed, closing the door behind them but not locking it. Morpheus was attempting to determine if there had been a change in de Ferrers' mental state — or if he had merely imagined it — when two soberly dressed porters entered and took away the body lying next to him.

They returned for a second body a few minutes later, and for de Ferrers a few minutes after that. Once again, Morpheus followed.

The *theater* the lecturer had mentioned turned out to be another, much larger vault, brightly lit and outfitted with benches at ever-increasing heights along the walls, in the style of an amphitheater. It was filled near to bursting with students numbering well over a hundred, their excited murmurs echoing off the stone walls.

Their daydreams hit Morpheus at the same moment as their low-pitched voices, stopping him as effectively as a wall.

Bodies, lying cut open on wooden slabs… organs removed and sliced into pieces… skin and muscle flayed, revealing bone and nerve and gristle.

Air whooshed from Morpheus' lungs in a startled hiss, for all that he did not need to breathe. The theater was filled with humans who would disassemble a corpse as one might attempt to disassemble a clever puzzle box, in hopes of uncovering its inner workings.

And Hugh de Ferrers was a man who could not die.

FIFTEEN

1821 A.D.

THE GRIZZLED human doctor — *Barclay* — stood by, rolling up his sleeves with deliberation as the porters arranged de Ferrers on one of the slabs in the center of the amphitheater and pulled back the sheet covering him.

The immortal man lay naked, fully exposed beneath the rapt gazes of the onlookers. Barclay immediately began to expound on the nature of traumatic injury, gesturing to various wounds on the three corpses as he described the effects of such damage on a living body. Beside him stood a small table holding a metal tray, laden with butcher's blades, hooks, and probes.

Morpheus stood just outside the edges of perception, lost in the shadows at the top of the stairs — his thoughts racing. The rage was back, but this was not a cell holding a few injured soldiers inside a French prison, or a handful of uneducated peasants chasing a witch. To send hundreds of humans to sleep in the middle of an institution of higher learning would not go unnoticed.

These were educated men. *Inquisitive* men, who sought answers to life's mysteries. If Morpheus dared interfere in the Sublunary on such a scale, reports of his actions would get back to those who watched for such things. More importantly, the reports of his interference would almost certainly get back to Phobetor, who would be quick to use the information against him in their ongoing skirmishes.

De Ferrers would live, no matter what was done to him.

He would live… until he asked for death.

What would be done with his remains once these *anatomists* were finished with him? Would they be buried? Burned? Taken to the nearest woods and thrown to the wild animals? Could any human survive such an experience and remain sane?

"We will begin with a standard Y-shaped incision into the torso," Barclay was saying. He chose a wicked-looking curved blade from the metal tray — lifting it and turning so that everyone in the theater could see the choice of tool.

His decision was made in the space of a human heartbeat. Morpheus manifested fully in the waking world. He reached within and stretched out his powers, those students nearest to his perch at the top of the stairs immediately nodding off as his aura touched them.

In the same instant, his delicate connection with de Ferrers' consciousness flared into life like a supernova. The human's mind flailed, enveloped in a nightmare that was all the more visceral for its close connection to reality. He gasped, his arms and legs thrashing as he tried to fight off the enemy swords coming at him inside his fever dream, unaware of the blade poised over him in the waking world.

The fast-expanding sphere of power around Morpheus collapsed like a popping bubble. He lunged through the between spaces separating him from de Ferrers as both Barclay and the immortal screamed in terror. Barclay stumbled backward, his surgical blade clattering to the stone floor. De

Ferrers scrambled in the opposite direction and promptly fell off the edge of the slab.

Morpheus materialized at his side, crouching over him protectively. Perhaps a more earthbound method of approach down the stairs would have been wiser, but somehow, he couldn't bring himself to care.

"This man is alive!" he roared, his voice echoing eerily around the massive vault. Only after the words had passed his lips did he register their sheer inanity. Everyone in the amphitheater could see perfectly well that de Ferrers was alive.

Barclay had landed in a heap among the students seated along the first row of benches. They set him back on his feet, though he seemed none too steady. Morpheus glared daggers at the surgeon, only dragging his burning gaze away when a shaking hand landed on his wrist.

He turned to the pale, shuddering form on the floor. De Ferrers' skin was as cold as the grave. His left temple was a mass of bruising. His lips, an unpleasant grayish blue.

"Stranger," he rasped. "Morpheus? Wh-what happened? Where am I?"

The evidence of lucidity — of *recognition* — loosened something inside Morpheus' ribcage. Logistics began to intrude into his awareness, as he recognized this new opportunity to extract them both from the situation in a way the humans would find largely explicable.

"There has been a misunderstanding," Morpheus told him, pitching his voice low. "Do not fear. All will be well."

De Ferrers gaped at him. "Easy for you to say! You're not the one f-freezing his naked b-bollocks off in the middle of a... a..." He looked around wildly. "What the hell *is* this place?"

Morpheus removed his coat once more, helping de Ferrers wrap it around himself. He spared a bit of power to give the fabric the illusion of being as warm as possible. "A temple of *learning*." He spat the final word, his gaze once more falling on Barclay.

The lecturer had crept closer during the brief exchange. "I say! What is the meaning of this?" he blustered, as though he hadn't been the one poised to slash a blade into the flesh of the man now shivering on the flagstones.

"This man is *alive*," Morpheus repeated, more quietly this time. Casting about for a story that these humans might find plausible, he continued, "He was caught up in the Cowgate protests and injured during the fray. I have been searching for him since I realized he was missing. I was told that some of the bodies might have ended up here."

"*Bodies*?" de Ferrers yelped, his attention falling on the other two occupied slabs. He cringed away, clearly realizing that he'd been similarly arranged for display.

Morpheus didn't let his unblinking stare at Barclay so much as flicker. "As I said, there has been a *misunderstanding*."

The lecturer blanched, then flushed. He cleared his throat loudly. "Yes," he agreed hoarsely. "A misunderstanding. It's... it's the kind of mistake anyone might have made, of course. You must be able to see that."

"*Quite,*" Morpheus said, the word wreathed in ice.

Barclay's lips worked for a moment as he sought a response.

When it took too long, Morpheus gave him one. "You will fetch a hot drink and a bowl of hearty broth for this man, along with clothing to replace what was stolen from him by your so-called *resurrection men.* You will supply money for a hackney carriage to return him to his home. You will also supply an apology."

The theater held its collective breath—a strange sort of echoing silence ricocheting around the vault.

Barclay looked between Morpheus and de Ferrers, his expression uncertain. "The university cannot be held responsible for—"

"You will be responsible to *me!*" Morpheus thundered, looking up from his kneeling position.

Barclay went as pale as a ghost and stumbled back a step. De Ferrers' hand closed on Morpheus' wrist again. His fingers were still shaking with cold, or reaction, or both.

"Morpheus," he murmured. "Your *eyes.*"

Morpheus blinked, becoming aware that shadows had begun to rise ominously around the edges of the vault, swallowing the light of lanterns as the darker aspect of his power slipped its bonds. With effort, he recalled it, forcing the darkness back inside his assumed physical form. The hand on his wrist relaxed.

It mattered not—his purpose had been achieved.

Trembling almost as hard as de Ferrers, Barclay turned to a student near the door at the top of the amphitheater. "You! Fetch McCready! This is his responsibility, so he can deal with it!" His gaze flicked nervously to Morpheus, and away again. "Tell the lad to provide this unfortunate gentleman with whatever he needs."

"And your apology?" Morpheus said icily.

"Mate, I don't need an apology," de Ferrers hissed. "Though a shirt would be nice."

Barclay, still flushed bright red, straightened his spine. "I apologize profusely, Mister…"

"Fergusson," de Ferrers offered tiredly. "Ta."

"I will put new procedures in place immediately to prevent any future occurrences like this," Barclay continued in stiff tones.

"Wonderful," de Ferrers told him. "Good luck with that."

Clutching the borrowed coat around himself, the human allowed Morpheus to lever him to unsteady feet, eyeing the narrow staircase leading up to the door with a heartfelt sigh.

✦

Two hours later, Morpheus and de Ferrers were clattering down the road in a rented hackney coach, heading for the rooms the human kept in a lodging house near an area called Grassmarket Square.

At his companion's request, Morpheus had related a brief outline of the previous twenty-four hours' events. De Ferrers, dressed in ill-fitting clothing presumably acquired from some of the students, had listened with an increasingly appalled expression.

"Well, that certainly could have been nasty," he said, once the tale was finished. He paused, frowning at Morpheus. "Would you *really* have put all those people to sleep in the middle of a university?"

"I would not have allowed you to come to further harm."

The words did nothing to clear the furrow between de Ferrers' thick eyebrows. He continued to stare at Morpheus as though attempting to see inside his skull. After a long stretch of silence, he sighed, slumping against the padded seat.

"That's how I guessed who you were, you know," he said, fiddling with a loose seam on his borrowed trousers. "That, and your brother, of course. 'Timor,' Latin for fear. And 'Iridaceae' could be Iris, one of the messengers of the gods. There were three brothers in Ovid's *Metamorphoses* — Phobetor, Phantasos, and Morpheus. Phobetor means 'Frightener,' so that one's pretty obvious. Though I was actually leaning toward you being Phantasos, at first."

Morpheus raised an eyebrow. "Why?" he asked, bewildered — thinking of his brother, whose incomparable beauty both inspired and reflected the fantasies of mortals.

De Ferrers flushed scarlet. "Just a guess, really," he muttered. Clearing his throat, he continued, "But then I remembered the way everyone fell asleep in

1621. Bit of a giveaway when I stopped and thought about it properly."

"You seem very sure of yourself," Morpheus said, oddly off-balance at the prospect of being known in such a way by a denizen of the Sublunary.

De Ferrers' crooked smile grew sardonic. "Don't worry. I'm not expecting you to confirm it. Or to tell me a single damned thing about yourself, for that matter."

Morpheus, as predicted, had nothing to say to that.

The silence stretched, expectant. When it was clear he wouldn't break it, de Ferrers let out a slow sigh. "Right. Anyway, thanks for not letting those maniacs slice me open. I don't like to think how that would have gone."

Morpheus contemplated that for a moment.

"Perhaps the next century will be less trying," he offered.

"One can only hope," de Ferrers agreed.

SIXTEEN

1921 A.D.

THE NEXT CENTURY did not end up being less trying than 1821 had been. Rather the opposite, in fact.

Hugh stood in the shadow of a doorway along Fifth Avenue on Easter Sunday of 1921, watching the great and the good of New York City pour out of church services. They crowded into the street for what had become an informal holiday parade over the years. From what he'd been told, it was a tradition that had sprung up in the wake of the American Civil War, decades earlier. Part celebration and part fashion show, the city's rich residents used it as an excuse to flaunt their wealth in the form of haute couture.

Unlike the steady stream of humanity promenading along the street, Hugh was not wearing his Sunday best, nor had he come from church. He'd barely managed to convince himself to leave his gloomy apartment — a silent, internal argument that had become a recurring theme in his life over the past three years.

He flinched violently when a tall, slender figure in a well-cut suit and top hat materialized at his side, despite the fact that he'd been expecting such a sudden appearance.

"Hello, Morpheus," he greeted, his voice raspy with disuse.

Hugh's stranger—if he could still be called that—tilted his head curiously as he eyed the sea of humanity forming before them.

"Many of these hats are patently ridiculous," said the man who was probably a minor Greco-Roman god. "When humans dream of headwear, it doesn't remotely resemble… *this*." He frowned, as though the presence of so many garishly dyed faux flowers and ostrich feathers was a personal affront to his delicate sensibilities.

"They're Easter bonnets," Hugh said, as patiently as he could manage. "For the purposes of this parade, the fact that they're ridiculous is more or less the point. It's… well, have you ever seen birds showing off their plumage as part of a mating dance? It's like that, only the plumage is either fake, or stolen from real birds."

"I see," Morpheus said, in a tone that clearly managed to convey the opposite.

Hugh sighed.

Down the street, a marching band had struck up a lively tune, to the delight of the impromptu parade-goers. Hugh tried to ignore the ungodly racket as they approached along the center of the street, realizing too late that his choice of meeting place had been a poor one. He could barely hear himself think, much less carry on a private conversation with another person.

The band had nearly reached them when a mustachioed fellow with a huge bass drum strapped to his chest attacked his instrument with a particular rhythm like mortars falling in a trench.

Boom-a-boom-a-boom-BOOM.

And just like that, Hugh was no longer standing along a city street in Manhattan. His surroundings swam, coalescing into a nightmare landscape of mud and blood and endless, endless gray. Bullets flew. Shells whistled through the air. The screams of dying men echoed in his ears. His chest seized up, constricted by the memory of vaporous gas clouds pouring over the edges of a trench like dense, London fog.

A hand closed around his bicep, and the image dispersed into wisps of green chlorine mist that blew away on the breeze. Morpheus was looking at him, staring into Hugh's face with his striking ice-blue gaze surrounded by creeping shadows. The darkness seemed to pour out from his eyes, much as it had done in an Edinburgh dissection theater in 1821.

Hugh tried to draw enough breath to speak, only to choke on the air as though it were poison. He realized with an unpleasant jolt that his limbs were shaking violently.

The hand tightened on his arm. The shadows receded, for all that they still lurked at the edges of the unseen, playing beneath his companion's pale skin.

"I recognize this vision," Morpheus said. "I've seen it many times within the minds of men, over these last few years. Come, we will go someplace more peaceful."

Hugh cursed his own weakness, the Germans, and whoever had invented marching bands. Putting one foot in front of the other, he allowed himself to be led along the edges of the crowd, moving against the flow as they hugged the front walls of buildings.

Several city blocks later, the familiar marble arch marking the entrance to Washington Square Park loomed ahead. Beyond it lay green grass, trees, and relative quiet, since most of the Fifth Avenue crowd were heading in the other direction, toward Central Park and the fashionable restaurants of the Upper West Side.

The area was far from deserted, but those who'd sought it out had done so for the same reason as he and Morpheus had done—for a bit of peace. Morpheus led the way to an empty bench near a bronze statue of Giuseppe Girabaldi, a historical figure Hugh thought he should probably know about but didn't.

Once they were seated, Morpheus turned toward him, their knees an inch apart. "There was a war," he prompted. "Tell me about it."

Hugh made a strangled sound that was probably trying to be a laugh.

"A war," he echoed. "A *war*. I've seen war, Morpheus. This wasn't a *war*. This was the end of days."

Morpheus' brow furrowed. His gaze flickered to the peaceful spring day... the green of the park. "I assure you; it was not."

Anger bubbled up beneath Hugh's lungs, and this, too, was familiar. *Shell shock*, the doctors called it, shaking their heads and tutting sadly. *Nothing to be done except take a few days' rest, soldier—and then you can be sent back to the front lines.*

"You weren't there." His voice shook. It took two tries to clasp his hands tightly in his lap so he could control their trembling. "You didn't see the tanks. The guns. The *gas*." He swallowed. The bobbing motion of his Adam's apple felt like razor blades going down. "I was a conchie—that's what they call conscientious objectors. They made me a stretcher-bearer. It was either that or prison."

"You aided the wounded?" Morpheus asked softly, his resonant steel-velvet voice unaccountably gentled.

"They sent us into hails of machine gun fire and mortar rounds to retrieve fallen soldiers." Hugh's eyes lost focus as he struggled not to disappear into the memory of sucking mud and explosions. "Sometimes we'd risk our lives pulling some poor sod out of the muck, drag him back to the nearest dressing station through enemy shelling and tangles of barbed wire, only to find out that he'd already died on the stretcher."

His companion watched Hugh with that luminous blue gaze, not interrupting the words that suddenly wanted to pour from him like water from a broken dam.

"Did you know that phosgene gas poisoning doesn't show up for twenty-four hours? They'd send a regiment back to the trenches, seemingly unhurt, only for the entire lot of them to collapse the following day with their lungs bubbling away, burned from the inside."

He gulped gracelessly, trying to wet his throat. "You can't see the stuff—not like chlorine or mustard gas. It's invisible, but it smells like musty grass. I tried to go back to horseshoeing, after the war ended. There's still demand for it, even with these new-fangled *automobiles* taking over the roads. But every time I caught a whiff of moldy hay, it catapulted me straight back to Ypres. So, I moved here, where everything's stone and concrete and steam engines. No mud. No musty hay." He let out a bitter laugh. "Just the occasional unexpected marching band drummer."

Silence reigned for a long moment.

"I did not know," Morpheus said eventually. "You never dreamed of it. If you had, I would have eased your nightmares."

The old, bitter anger that had been simmering in Hugh's gut surged higher.

"I never dreamed of it because *I don't fucking sleep!*" he snapped. "An hour here. An hour there. That's all. I've tried drinking myself into a stupor. I've tried laudanum, morphine, heroin. *Nothing fucking helps!*"

Morpheus reared back an inch, as though Hugh had raised a hand to strike him. For some reason, *that* was the thing that finally made his temper boil over.

Hugh's tone went ice cold, to match his frozen soul. "Fifty. *Million.* Dead. War... plague... destruction on a scale never seen before. And you, a fucking *god*! We both know it. How *dare* you sit there talking about one man's bad dreams, when your kind *let this happen*. You didn't lift a finger. *You didn't even warn me what was coming!*"

And that was the thing, wasn't it? That sense of betrayal, that his oldest acquaintance—his oldest friend?—would let him walk blindly into hell without a word of warning. *Perhaps the next century will be less trying*, Morpheus had said blithely. The memory made Hugh want to throw up.

"Prophecy is not my function," Morpheus said, his expression grown stony in the face of Hugh's vitriol. "Look to your own kind if you seek to lay blame. Humanity makes its choices and buries its own dead."

"Then what the hell are you good for?" Hugh shouted, trembling for a different reason now. Several passersby turned alarmed looks in his direction, increasing their pace to get away from the English madman making a scene on a park bench.

His companion's face might as well have been carved from pale marble. "If you presume to know me, then you know the answer to that question as well." He rose from his seat. "Perhaps it would be best if I take my leave now."

Hugh rose to mirror him, fists clenched, ignoring the way his knees shook. "Oh, yeah? Why don't you fuck off for good, then?" His voice rose to an unsteady pitch. "Seven hundred years, and I still have no idea what you even want with me! Well, I'm done with you, do you hear? *Done!*"

The horrible wrongness of the words lodged in Hugh's throat, but they'd already escaped into the world. The two of them stood arrested for an interminable moment, staring each other down.

Morpheus blinked himself free first, his spine as straight as a rail. "So it appears," he said evenly, before turning and walking away.

Hugh's vision wavered, his inner voice screaming at him to follow, to grab Morpheus by the shoulder and spin him around... to keep him from leaving, to continue the argument… he wasn't sure which. But when he dragged his surroundings back into focus, the slender figure dressed in black was gone from view.

Hugh collapsed onto the bench and sat there for hours, staring at nothing—only dragging himself back to his rented rooms when the sun slid toward the western horizon.

That night, for the first time in more than four years, he slept soundly through the darkness and deep into the following morning.

He did not dream.

SEVENTEEN

1940 A.D.

THE YEAR WAS 1940 as it was reckoned in the Sublunary, and the humans were warring again. Or perhaps that was misleading, since the humans were *always* warring to some degree or another. This war, however, had the same flavor as the one that had chewed up Hugh de Ferrers and spat him out earlier in the century as grist for the military mill.

De Ferrers had made his desire not to see Morpheus again quite clear during their ill-fated meeting in 1921. That did not stop Morpheus from watching over his dreams. Nor had it stopped him from *appearing* in the human's dreams, frequently with very little in the way of clothing.

The contradiction was vexing.

Nevertheless, when de Ferrers' dreams turned to death and destruction, Morpheus did not allow his distress to escalate into chronic sleeplessness as it had before. He certainly owed the man that much care after so many centuries as his unwitting champion.

The distress of the collective unconscious had reached alarming levels — worse, even, than during the first Great War. Terror gripped humanity like a suffocating fist, and it sickened him to consider that Phobetor might have somehow fomented the carnage taking place in the waking realm.

If true, such a crime could not go unpunished. Yet the very laws his brother flouted constrained Morpheus from delving too deeply into the affairs of the mortals. How could he investigate Phobetor's culpability without interfering himself?

And so, he remained resigned to watching and waiting—while quietly ensuring that one immortal's waking suffering did not carry over into sleep. Meanwhile, if his brother ever made a misstep and revealed himself openly, Morpheus would be ready to step in.

There were higher powers in the universe than mere gods, after all.

———◆———

Meanwhile, on a windswept dock in the Amsterdam port of IJmuiden, Hugh stood next to the gangplank of the *SS Bodegraven*, urging his queue of frightened children to hurry aboard. He glanced over his shoulder, gauging the position of the line of approaching German planes, and turned back to the crying Jewish girl clutching a tiny, battered valise.

"Go on, sweetheart," he urged in fractured Dutch. "This boat will take you and the others to safety."

The air was thick with smoke from the burning oil tanks down the coast—set alight by the Dutch to prevent their valuable fuel from falling into German hands. If the approaching fighter planes were laden with bombs, this scene would soon turn into a bloodbath. He could only hope they were returning from a mission with empty cargo holds, their payloads already dropped elsewhere.

Hitler's forces had invaded the Netherlands the day before. This would be the last *Kindertransport* leaving Amsterdam, and possibly the last Dutch ship of any kind. Reports were that Rotherdam lay in ruins. By comparison, Amsterdam had fared better—but closing down the port would be a priority for the German forces.

Hugh had become aware of the Refugee Children's Movement not long after the deadly *Kristallnacht*, when thousands of Jews had been arrested or killed by Nazi forces during a night of destruction extending across Germany. While he refused to be hauled onto another battlefield after Ypres, he could at least help save a few innocents from a madman.

At first, the RCM had evacuated Jewish children directly from Austria and Germany. But as Hitler's army marched east, their rescue efforts had turned to Prague, then Warsaw, and now Amsterdam. The *SS Bodegraven* was bound for England, where the children would be transported to London and taken to either waiting foster families or temporary camps set up in local orphanages.

There, they would be safe. Mad as he was, Hitler wouldn't dare invade the British Isles. It would stretch his forces too thin, especially with Russia stirring on his eastern flank like a waking bear.

A figure appeared at the deck railing above him—the *Bodegraven*'s captain.

"We must leave!" he called. "There is no more time!"

The drone of approaching planes was growing louder.

"Go, go!" Hugh urged the last few children. "Hurry now! Show me how fast you can get up to the deck!"

Tiny, frightened faces scurried up the gangplank, some with a single piece of luggage, others with nothing more than a paper card attached to one wrist by a loop of twine. A name. A number. Nothing else but the clothes on their back.

When the last one had embarked, he followed them onto the deck. The *Bodegraven* was a simple cargo ship. The woman who'd organized this last-minute evacuation of seventy-four vulnerable souls had talked the captain into taking on the children out of the goodness of his heart. Now, his ship had become a target.

"Everyone, get under cover!" Hugh shouted, as the handful of RCM representatives herded their charges belowdecks.

One small boy clutching a ratty blanket stood unattended near the gangplank, crying loudly. Hugh scooped him up as the roar of engines reached a crescendo overhead, running for the nearest upturned rescue boat to use as cover.

"Put your hands over your ears," he said, as calmly and cheerfully as he could. Sucking in a breath, he curled his body over the boy's as machine-gun fire strafed the deck, sending splinters flying only a few feet from their hiding place.

Seconds ticked by, but no bombs followed. Hugh let out the breath he'd been holding and uncurled. "There," he said. "All over. Now, let's get you set up with a place to bunk, shall we?"

The boy looked up at him mutely, his tear-stained face ghostly pale.

That night, Hugh fell asleep in his borrowed canvas hammock to the sound of children whimpering in fear and hunger. He dreamed of a familiar idyllic glade, soft with grass and cushioning moss, and a faceless, comforting figure who stroked his head where it rested on a corded thigh. When he woke, he spared a thought for a god who apparently didn't care enough to stop humans killing each other in droves, but who still deigned to chase away the nightmares of a single, foolish man.

<hr>

Meanwhile, deep in an underground bunker west of London, Professor Frederick Rainey stared down at the damaged grimoire resting on his desk, trying to convince himself that it contained anything remotely useful to the British War Office.

Since being recruited from Cambridge, he'd been thrust into a secret project that would make even the most ambitious academic blanch—namely, coming up with effective countermeasures for the rumored occult weapons being developed by Germany's Third Reich.

As if guns and bombs weren't enough, Hitler was allegedly researching ways to weaponize demonology in advance of his anticipated offensive against France and the UK. And apparently, Frederick was supposed to stop him.

"This is insane," he muttered, closing the grimoire with a rustle of flaking paper.

Whatever resources you need, whatever the cost in either money or manpower, it's yours, his shadowy handler had informed him, before showing him down to the massive concrete warren that was to be his new domain.

And here he had sat for twelve hours every day since, rifling through ancient texts and dusty tomes in hopes of some sort of epiphany regarding a task which seemed by every rational measure to be impossible.

Time is of the essence. We have another specialist flying in to consult on the project.

Frederick hoped this mysterious specialist had some new insight to offer, because he'd never asked for this job. He also had no idea how one quit from a top-secret agency where no one except him seemed to have so much as a name, much less a rank or title.

When the specialist finally arrived, Frederick began to wish he hadn't.

"Professor Rainey," his handler greeted. "Allow me to introduce Doctor Timor. I trust the two of you will have a fruitful collaboration."

And then he'd gone, leaving Frederick alone with a man who was too tall and too angular, like a spider in human form. His presence prickled at Frederick's nerves like tiny, cold needles. When he spoke, his voice sounded like the rustling of wind through a graveyard.

"My dear Professor," he said. "It does appear you have rather a knotty problem to untangle."

Frederick cleared his throat, willing his answer to be steady and not a high-pitched squeak of fear.

"I suppose you could say that. I assume you've been briefed on the particulars?"

A slow smile spread over Timor's features. "Oh, I have indeed. And it just so happens, I may have a solution for you. What would you say if I told you there exists a creature with the power to destroy Hitler's army by poisoning their sleep?"

Frederick blinked. Was the man speaking of a demon, of the sort that the Germans were supposedly courting? "I... suppose I might ask how one would go about trapping such a powerful creature and binding it to our will."

The disconcerting smile widened. "As it happens, binding it in this realm is not so terribly difficult a thing." He swung a heavy knapsack off his shoulder. It clanked when it hit the desk. "At least, not if one has *these*."

Timor pulled out a set of heavy metal chains attached to golden shackles engraved with esoteric symbols. Frederick took an involuntary step back. The chains were glowing unnaturally beneath the harsh overhead lights.

He swallowed hard, forcing himself to move closer; to examine the engravings without touching the luminous metal.

"I... uh... I can see that these are no ordinary chains," he managed, "but that does not answer the question of how such a creature might be drawn here, much less overpowered long enough for the shackles to be utilized."

"How astute of you," said Timor, his raspy voice caressing the words. "As it happens, the shackles are only one part of the plan. Tell me,

Professor — what do you know of the practice of lucid dreaming?"

EIGHTEEN

1940 A.D.

IRIDACEAE TILTED HER head to one side, staring at a bizarre assemblage of humans gathered in Morpheus' palatial throne room. He watched her turn slowly in place to take them in, one by one.

"That's... certainly rather odd," she said eventually.

Morpheus nodded his agreement. "It is indeed."

He stood—observing his mysterious observers—with an elbow cupped in one hand, while his other hand worried thoughtfully at his chin. The humans had appeared around him in the palace, exactly like this, for the last several nights consecutively. A circle of thirteen young men, dressed in military uniforms, all staring at him with distant eyes, one arm raised to point directly at him.

On each successive night, they'd stood in their odd, accusatory formation for approximately twenty minutes—the average length of a human dream, as measured by the common unit of time in the Sublunary. They did not appear all at once, nor did they depart all at once. They flickered in one by one, although still within a short enough span that all were present for the bulk of the time. Then they flickered out randomly, returning to wakefulness or lighter, non-dreaming slumber.

It was perplexing in the extreme.

"How long has this been going on?" Iridaceae asked.

"This is the seventh night," he replied absently, noting with interest that none of the soldiers even seemed to register the presence of a naked, nubile young female at his side.

"Well? What does it mean?" his familiar demanded, her innate impatience coming to the fore. "What are you going to do about it?"

"I've no idea what it means," he said, walking slowly around the circle. The humans' dazed eyes tracked his movement, their pointing fingers following his progress from one man to the next. "And I haven't decided what to do about it. If anything."

"But they're *looking* at you," Iridaceae said, sounding rather disconcerted by the fact. "You're the god of dreams and nightmares. The only human who ever dreams of you directly is the furry one who likes to imagine you with your clothes off."

"He does have a name, Iridaceae," Morpheus chided, aware that de Ferrers' dreams about him since their unfortunate parting twenty years previous had been conflicted, at best.

"Yes, yes." She shrugged her shoulders as though resettling ruffled wing feathers and gestured at the nearest figure. "Shouldn't you follow one of these back to the Sublunary, just to see what's going on? The humans have been behaving *very* strangely for the past few years, after all."

She'd learned not to raise his ire by asking outright whether Phobetor was responsible for any of the inconceivable atrocities the humans had been visiting on each other of late. It was heavily implied, however.

And this was, quite transparently, something aimed at him in particular. It could hardly be called interference when he was being directly summoned.

"Perhaps so," he allowed.

Iridaceae clapped her hands in excitement. "Good! What do they wear down there these days? We need to hurry. They're starting to fade."

Indeed, three of the blank-faced soldiers had already disappeared. Another dissipated as Morpheus considered what he knew of the current style of garb in Western Europe, where it was currently night. After a moment's thought, he conjured drab boy's clothing for Iridaceae. His dark, flowing robed shifted into a sober suit jacket and trousers.

Six more of the figures had vanished in the interim.

"Come," he said, latching onto the consciousness of one of the stragglers. "Let us untangle this small mystery."

The young soldier hailed from a place called Portsmouth, and he dreamed of returning there after the war to rejoin his sweetheart. As the human slipped out of his dream state, Morpheus pulled himself and Iridaceae into the Sublunary with him. They materialized in a stark, underground space, all damp white walls and sharp edges. Thirteen low cots stood arrayed in a circle around them, occupied by the sleeping or newly awakened men who had invaded his throne room for the last week. They were strapped down to the metal bed frames. Every man wore a thick band around his head, which trailed wires to the floor and out of sight.

Beyond them stood a middle-aged man with a drawn, haggard expression and a rumpled white lab coat that looked like it had been worn for several days in a row without laundering. He was flanked on either side by two more soldiers, each holding a heavy firearm aimed directly at Morpheus and his familiar.

"That's him!" exclaimed the man in the lab coat. "Oh, my god! Fire! *Fire!*"

Morpheus took a surprised step back, instinctively caging Iridaceae behind him as one of the firearms exploded with a deafening crack. To his utter shock, a pellet of hot metal slammed into his left shoulder, penetrating skin, muscle, and bone in a flash of burning white agony.

It should not have been possible. He staggered, sudden fear for his all too vulnerable familiar lending him a surge of strength.

"Go!" he gasped. "Iridaceae, *fly!*"

With a terrified squawk, Iridaceae shifted into owl form and flapped upward. Morpheus channeled all of his remaining power and shoved her through the veil between realms, catapulting her back to the Night Lands. A second explosion of noise hit him at the same instant as another burning projectile. This one burst through his sternum and embedded itself in his heart.

Morpheus fell to his knees, clutching at the gaping hole with his good hand… staring at the blood pulsing through his fingers in stark disbelief. He opened his mouth to demand '*How?*', but no sound emerged beyond a strangled croak. Tendrils of magic wormed outward from the metal trapped inside him, binding him to his shattered physical form.

It was *old* magic. The kind that traveled through the years as whispers, lest the gods snuff it out before it could harm them. What was this kind of magic doing in a cold, sterile bunker full of soldiers?

Morpheus doubled over, physical shock sapping him of the ability to remain upright. The cots with their bound dreamers wavered in and out of focus, a red mist creeping in from the edges of his vision until it grew all-encompassing, blotting out everything else. The mist grew ever darker and more impenetrable, rendering him blind as well as mute.

He barely felt the impact of the cold concrete against his injured shoulder as he collapsed to the floor, unconscious.

———◆———

Across the Channel, in an overcrowded French Resistance safehouse hidden deep in the slums of Paris, Hugh de Ferrers jerked awake.

Heart pounding, he sat up, being careful not to wake the men and women sleeping on the floor around him. His hands shook as half-remembered images of bullets tearing into flesh on a muddy battlefield faded slowly into the depths of his consciousness.

It was the first nightmare he'd had since the war began.

A chill that had nothing to do with the lack of heat in the room trickled down the length of his spine.

It was *the first nightmare*.

The first since he'd sent his stranger—his *Morpheus*—away with harsh words and accusations. Not even a god's patience was infinite. Yet Hugh had hurled insults at the slight figure dressed in black; cursed him with all the vitriol his shattered mind could muster.

'Then what the hell are you good for?'

'I'm done with you, do you hear? Done!'

His angry words still echoed in the halls of memory. And despite it all, for the many long years since, the God of Nightmares had withheld his dark powers from one particular immortal idiot with a short temper and a long memory.

No more, it seemed. Morpheus had withdrawn his aid from his pathetic human experiment at last. And Hugh wasn't sure he'd ever be able to take another full breath without feeling the ache of it.

NINETEEN

1940 A.D.

IRIDACEAE TUMBLED into the throne room in a flurry of wings and feathers, her head spinning, her owl's heart fluttering in panic. She *knew* that noise… that sharp, unexpected *crack*. She had heard it in a thousand dreams at her master's side. The explosion of gunfire, so often accompanied by the bloom of blood and the stench of death.

Why had Morpheus not returned to the palace with her? Surely such human weapons could not touch a being like him. She shook herself off and hopped onto the back of the throne, waiting with bated breath for him to materialize in the space before her. He would be crackling with irritation at the ruse, ready to tear into whoever had orchestrated it.

Somewhere in the Sublunary, a human would spend the rest of its miserable life trapped in nightmares.

Morpheus did not appear.

She tried to reach out, following the thread they had traversed between the Night Lands and the waking realm. But without her master's power, she couldn't cross through the veil. Again and again, she flapped toward the spot where they had stood among the circle of dreaming soldiers. Again and again, she had to pull up sharply or risk flying headfirst into the throne room wall.

Next, she landed on the floor and tried to transform into her human body.

Nothing happened.

Her panic rose higher. How could she convey what had befallen Morpheus if she couldn't speak? He needed help. She was certain of it. Never in a thousand years had she heard the kind of fear in his voice as when he'd told her to fly away… to leave him.

She had to do something.

Gathering herself, she flapped her wings and darted down the hallway leading to the palace entrance—heading toward Tartarus, where Morpheus' uncle might be found when his duties allowed.

———◆———

Pain was the first sensation to register as Morpheus' awareness returned from wherever it had fled. Time had passed without his knowledge—a sensation completely alien to him.

He was naked except for some scratchy material that had been tied around his hips like a loincloth, presumably as a nod to modesty. Evidently, he'd lost control of the magic manifesting his clothing—another thing he'd never experienced before.

His chest and shoulder still throbbed a protest at the metal lodged inside his body. He attempted to reach out with his mind—to know the inner lives of the creatures swarming around him like ants. Their dreams, their nightmares, their hopes.

There was nothing. Only blankness beyond the bounds of his battered physical form. Blinking his eyes against the brutal white glare surrounding him, he found himself lying face-down with his cheek pressed against gritty concrete. As his vision swam fully into focus, he saw his own wrist, encased in a golden manacle inscribed with symbols of power. His eyes followed a length of heavy chain, glowing with magic of its own, which stretched from the manacle to a massive metal ring bolted into the concrete floor.

When he tried to turn his head to check his other wrist, he was hindered by a choking weight encircling his neck. Another chain scraped against the floor as he moved. A metal collar.

Rage welled inside his ravaged chest.

They had *collared* him.

Him! A *god*, who could have plunged every single one of them into nightmares the likes of which would drive them to madness and death.

But he could do none of those things now. He had been *chained*. By *humans*.

It was impossible. These simple creatures should not have had access to this kind of magic. The shackles... he recognized them, or he thought he did. Thanatus had sometimes used such manacles to bind miscreants inside his realm of Tartarus. Famously, the embodiment of death had once been tricked into them himself by Sisyphus, a human troublemaker who'd always believed he was cleverer than the gods.

In this case, he *had* been cleverer. Sisyphus had earned his eventual punishment in the Night Lands, but not before he'd bested Thanatus and trapped him in his own realm for months—with these chains, or ones very like them.

Thanatus had only escaped after one of the other gods had realized that nothing in the Sublunary was dying and gone to check on him. His formidable uncle, who held far more power than Morpheus had ever aspired to, had been unable to free himself. An unaccustomed chill spread through his weakened body, radiating outward from the cold metal circling his wrists and throat.

Was this… *fear*?

With an effort of will, Morpheus rolled his weight onto his uninjured arm and pushed up, shuffling his knees under him. The chains jerked him to a stop before he could fully straighten into a kneeling position, leaving his head bowed and his arms stretched outward as if in supplication.

Fresh anger at the indignity of the position chased away some of the chill of dread.

Coiling his trembling muscles in readiness, he heaved upward, jerking at his bonds. The bolts embedded in the concrete floor creaked, but they did not give. The chains glowed brighter, as though drawing power from his struggles. His shackles burned like ice against the skin of his neck and wrists.

A low, animal noise of frustration rumbled up from his chest.

Legs clad in brown wool trousers appeared in his field of vision, coming to a stop directly in front of him. He strained to look up, meeting the gaze of the careworn human with his wrinkled face and graying hair, wearing his long, white coat.

Morpheus bared his teeth in a snarl.

"You're awake," said the human. His tone was nervous, and he fiddled with a metal clipboard held cradled in his hands. "That's good. I'm sorry for… all this." He gestured with the clipboard in a motion that was clearly intended to encompass the chains and the bullets, as well as the general degradation of being shackled to the floor while wearing nothing but a scratchy woolen breechcloth.

"*Release me*," Morpheus growled, taken aback when his voice didn't send shudders through the concrete and drop the humans to their knees in horror. Indeed, the words were a mere rasp against his dry throat.

"I'm afraid I can't do that unless you agree to help us," said the man. His fiddling increased in tempo, and beads of sweat popped out on his forehead. "We know how powerful you are. And… er… the individual who assisted with the plans to draw you here and bind you was somewhat less forthcoming about what would happen after we captured you."

"What have you done to me?" Morpheus demanded, feeling the buried projectile in his heart shift and tear deeper with every movement.

"I'm afraid you're quite trapped," said the man, almost apologetically. "You've been shot twice with bullets inscribed with a series of binding pentacles on the metal jackets. Very fine workmanship We had to bring in a rather famous jeweler to do the engraving. Additionally, these chains are imbued with enough power to imprison… your kind."

"My *kind*?" Morpheus echoed, his tone growing dangerous.

"Demons," the human said.

The ignobility of being mistaken for such a low creature was almost worse than the shackles.

Almost.

"We know you can control dreams and night-mares," his captor went on. "We need you to control the dreams of a specific group of people. Or, failing that, of a specific man. Adolf Hitler. Maybe you've, ah, heard of him? From what we've learned, he's been seeking to leverage demonic powers of his own for almost a year now."

Morpheus only glared at him.

The human swallowed audibly. "So, er, I'll leave you to think about my offer. We can talk more tomorrow. Again, I'm truly sorry for the conditions. But you must understand, we need you. Millions of lives are at stake. Please think about it."

And then he left.

Morpheus knelt on the gritty floor, straining against the confinement of his bonds. Around him, brisk footsteps echoed through the underground bunker, but no other humans approached him. His mind circled restlessly through the handful of relevant facts.

Someone had told these men how to lure him here and bind him.

That same someone had provided his captors with knowledge and artifacts to which they should *in no way* have access.

Their method of restraining him was painfully effective.

None of these facts changed the reality of his situation. Even though the idea of kneeling here like some abject prisoner burned in his veins like acid, Morpheus settled in to wait for whatever happened next.

———◆———

In the days and weeks that followed, it became painfully clear that this human with his clipboard and his wrinkled white lab coat had absolutely no idea what to do with the tiger he'd caught by the tail.

The man's co-conspirator—and Morpheus had his own thoughts as to the identity of that individual—had given him only enough information to be dangerous. Morpheus had learned that his captor's name was Rainey, and that he was a professor, a man of letters. He'd further surmised that Rainey was not working with the military by choice, even though he appeared unwilling or unable to protest his involuntary conscription.

At some point, it had occurred to Rainey that *he* was the one in the trap. He dared not free Morpheus from the magic binding him, for fear of Morpheus' power. Rainey thought him a demon, and he knew he could not trust such a creature to refrain from taking revenge on its tormentors.

On the other hand, Morpheus was useless to him so long as his powers were constrained. He could hardly be expected to drive this 'Hitler' and his supporters mad when he was too weakened to do so much as stand.

And so, the stalemate dragged on.

Anger churned bitterly in Morpheus' stomach, even as his heart burned and blistered around the pentacle-inscribed bullet. His shoulder ached. Cold suffused him, radiating outward from the golden shackles.

Some of his anger was for Rainey and the nameless, blank-faced soldiers populating this featureless place. Most was reserved for the one who had led Rainey down this path, to the dead end that now confronted him.

Rainey had been, for the most part, the picture of polite contrition. In an attempt to gain some sort of rapport with his stoic captive, the human had explained his methods for luring Morpheus to this place—thirteen soldiers trained in a practice recently dubbed 'lucid dreaming' by a Dutch psychiatrist. The men had been shown an obscure classical painting of a palace throne room with its walls covered in mirrors of various shapes and sizes, along with a portrait in miniature that bore an uncanny resemblance to Morpheus. After much practice, all thirteen soldiers were able to call up that setting in dreams and visit it.

Rainey had even shown Morpheus the portrait, which was a strikingly accurate portrayal.

Morpheus had known of the sixteenth-century painting of his throne room, and he cursed himself for not having destroyed it at some point during the intervening years. It was the work of a talented but relatively unknown madwoman, long dead—one who had also possessed the gift of self-aware dreaming.

The portrait's provenance, by contrast, was a mystery. He could think of only one likely candidate who might have commissioned it or painted it himself, and if so, it was a harsh blow indeed.

Morpheus stopped speaking altogether on the third day. He was a god; he would not bargain or cajole for his release with creatures whose bones would rot to dust before his eyes as the years marched past.

Rainey continued to talk to him, nevertheless—sometimes for hours at a time. An endless litany of atrocities committed by Hitler and his forces… moral defense of his own actions… emotional pleas for help that would ultimately keep his children and grandchildren safe from the German war machine.

None of it moved Morpheus to break his self-imposed silence.

Men with stiff shoulders and more baubles on their drab military uniforms came and went, staring at him with calculating eyes. Sometimes they berated Rainey for his lack of progress. Sometimes they made suggestions for methods of torture or other coercion to gain Morpheus' cooperation.

"Put a few whip marks across that pale back or throw him in a vat of ice water for an hour or two. He'll soon get with the program."

"Due respect, sir—but the creature has had an armor-piercing bullet lodged in his heart for more than a month. I'm not sure a cold bath would have much impact."

Back and forth it went, with Rainey growing more and more desperate as the weeks rolled on, yielding no progress in their stalemate.

And then, one night, the bombs began to fall.

TWENTY

1940 A.D.

IRIDACEAE FLAPPED AROUND the rough wooden table where Thanatus was sharing a bottle of wine with Phantasos. Her master's younger brother, who normally chose to present himself as a beautiful youth with wild curls of honey-blond hair, waved a hand at her irritably.

"What's *wrong* with the creature?" he asked in a plaintive voice. "Why will she not leave us in peace? Shoo! *Shoo!*"

"Morpheus has abandoned her, it seems," Thanatus said reflectively, his hard black eyes following Iridaceae as she circled the table. "Without his power, she is trapped. So, she behaves like all trapped animals—by panicking."

Frustration made her want to scratch and peck at his face, but she wasn't quite *that* far gone yet, fortunately for her continued existence.

"Hmm," Phantasos mused. "She's not the only thing my taciturn brother has abandoned. It's increasingly apparent that he's deserted his duties altogether. Does no one know where he is?"

Iridaceae wanted to scream. She contented herself with dive-bombing the infuriating godling's artfully disheveled hair. He hissed in irritation and batted a hand at her.

"Apparently not," Thanatus replied. "I can detect no trace of him in either the Night Lands or the Sublunary. He appears to be in hiding."

He's not hiding, you fool! Iridaceae flapped between them, narrowly missing the wine bottle. *He's been captured!*

It was the only possible explanation. If her master had been able to return to the palace, he would have done so. The fear in his voice as he'd ordered her away to safety still echoed in her memory like warning bells.

"Have you asked Phobetor?" Phantasos inquired, watching Iridaceae with a wary eye.

Thanatus' expression turned sour. "Phobetor prefers his games in the human realm to our company, these days. He's hardly ever here."

Phantasos made a considering noise. "Yes. About that. It's not really... *allowed,* is it? The humans have become quite unruly recently."

The god of death looked even unhappier than before. "Interference is interference. I can hardly wade in and start throwing my power around in an attempt to rein in Phobetor. I'd be just as bad as he is."

Phantasos shot him a sly look. "And whatever's happening down there, it's certainly providing you with a steady stream of dying souls, eh?"

Thanatus raised a dark eyebrow. "Just as it's providing you with a steady supply of humans desperate to fantasize about better conditions and happier times. Especially with their dreams disrupted, thanks to your brother's dereliction."

A slow smile spread across the younger god's lovely face. "Why, yes. And so it is."

Iridaceae let out a hooting cry of fury and knocked the wine bottle into Phantasos' lap before flying off in a huff.

————◆————

Chaos erupted in the underground bunker where Morpheus crouched, chained and helpless. The ground shook with nearby explosions. Chunks of concrete fell from the ceiling, releasing clouds of debris as they crashed to the heaving floor.

"Bunker buster bombs!" someone cried. "Take cover! *Take cover!*"

Elsewhere, humans were screaming... crying out for help. Sobs rent the dust-choked air.

Morpheus clenched his jaw, willing the concrete around the bolts of his imprisonment to crack. A white-coated figure appeared from the billowing dust, staggering toward him.

Rainey's face was a study in terror. He dropped his ever-present clipboard in favor of fumbling in his coat pocket.

"I'm sorry," he cried. "I'm so sorry, demon! I'll release you... you can go back to wherever you came fr—"

A steel beam screamed under the strain and collapsed, crushing him. A small, golden key skidded free from his grip, coming to rest a few inches from fingers that spasmed convulsively and then went still.

Morpheus stared blankly at the tiny piece of metal lying several feet away, hopelessly out of his reach.

The last surviving lights flickered and went out, plunging the underground complex into darkness. A boulder-sized hunk of concrete slammed into his injured shoulder and rolled off, sending agony through him as the pentacle-inscribed bullet shifted within his flesh.

More explosions shuddered through the failing structure. The screams continued. Human lungs gradually failed as the choking dust grew thicker. The cries of distress faded to weak coughing and eventually, to silence. Morpheus stared wide-eyed into gray nothingness—all his senses focused on the location where the key had fallen.

He strained against his chains.

The bolts held.

For the first time in his imprisonment—the first time in his *existence*—claustrophobia clawed at his gut like crawling insects. The concrete dust was a physical presence brushing against his skin from all directions. In the absence of light, it felt like being encased in a smothering blanket that clung to him from head to foot.

His muscles trembled with strain. Distantly, another section of the ceiling collapsed with a shattering crash. The steel reinforcements groaned beneath their shifting load. Occasionally, the low moan of an injured human emerged from the depths of the bunker... growing less and less frequent as minutes passed, then hours.

The dust settled slowly, only to billow up again when some new part of the structure collapsed. Morpheus crouched, trapped among the destruction by his chains, his body coated in the fine, gray powder. Eventually, the remains of the bunker achieved a state of fragile equilibrium, everything descending into stillness.

He continued to stare toward the last resting place of the key, unseeing. Hours passed. A day. More.

The sound of muffled voices filtered in to him… pickaxes against rubble.

More time passed.

The voices grew clearer. Beams of light penetrated the blank grayness, moving crazily to and fro.

"Search for survivors. Do *not* approach the experimental subject, on pain of court martial."

Boot steps shuffled among the debris, soldiers calling out to each other as they identified crushed and asphyxiated bodies. Morpheus winced as one of the beams of light played over him, briefly blinding him.

A sharp intake of breath reached his ears from the vicinity of the light source.

"S-sir?" The voice sounded both young and startled. "The experimental subject is alive. It's… it's a *man*, sir!"

A second pair of footsteps approached, coming to a halt behind the glare of the beam. "I assure you, corporal—it is not. The higher-ups have decreed the creature too dangerous to release. Its bonds appear secure, thankfully. It will remain confined here until a safe means of disposing of it can be determined. Resume your search."

The second set of footsteps moved away, but the beam remained on Morpheus for another few seconds. Then it dipped to the floor, playing over the chains and heavy bolts. Something glinted, a tiny reflection in a sea of gray.

The light illuminated the golden key, its inner glow cutting through the coating of grit. No longer blinded, Morpheus looked up, meeting wide eyes set in the narrow face of a boy barely approaching manhood.

The young soldier stared at him for a long moment, his mouth hanging open. Morpheus tried to draw breath to speak, to demand release—only to find that the thick coating of dust in his throat had rendered him voiceless.

The corporal glanced around furtively, then ducked and swept the key into his free hand, making it disappear inside one of his pockets in an instant. Before Morpheus could manage more than an abortive jerk toward his only chance at freedom, the human hurried back toward his fellows... returning to the grim search for the dead.

Over the following hours, crews pulled corpses out of the rubble and carted them away on stretchers, giving the chained *experimental subject* a wide and wary berth.

"That's the last of the ones we can get without risking bringing the whole bunker down on our heads, sir," said a gruff voice.

"Very good," replied the officer who appeared to be in charge. "Make sure everyone's clear and blow the entrance. I want this facility sealed up tight."

Morpheus jerked against his bonds, forcing a wordless, choked animal noise past his uncooperative throat. Bellowed orders rang back and forth, drowning out his pathetic cry. The beams of light disappeared one by one as the soldiers retreated from the destroyed facility, until it was once more plunged into tomblike darkness.

Morpheus knelt, shaking with the need to be on the other side of that entrance—but helpless to move. His flesh-caged heart thudded against his ribs, each fluttering beat scraping against the stubborn bullet lodged inside it like an anchor.

Minutes ticked by in slow motion.

A series of thundering booms shuddered through the remains of the bunker. The familiar sound of collapsing steel and concrete rang in his ears once more. New dust billowed through the echoing space, mixing with the old as another section of the ceiling caved in. Once again, the groan of strained supports gradually subsided. The dust settled.

Silence fell, leaving Morpheus alone in the cold darkness.

TWENTY-ONE

2021 A.D.

WHAT ONCE WAS OLD was new again. Hugh had started his life as a farrier and a blacksmith, shoeing the horses of soldiers and plowmen alike. Now, as the world seemed poised to slide into the abyss of madness, he was a farrier and a blacksmith once more.

The year 2021 had started unseasonably warm in the south of England, but, as February turned to March, winter chill was reclaiming its domain. It wasn't a pleasant time to have an outdoor job… or even a job that took place largely inside damp, unheated barns. However, Hugh had found it was easier to ignore the insanity creeping across the globe in rural areas like this.

Hugh kept a cottage in the woods south of Long Sutton, hidden away among the trees from the nearby farms and landed gentry, nestled at the end of a narrow, one-lane road. The little house was younger than Hugh, but only by a couple hundred years. It had been in sad shape when he'd purchased it, but utilizing the old skills he'd honed during the first few centuries of his life was another way Hugh kept himself distracted from everything else.

He didn't have a telly, or a radio, or the internet. With the current state of humanity, he'd rather stab himself in the eye with a rusty fork than use any of those things. He owned a mobile phone because that was the easiest way for his clients to contact him, but that was all he used it for. His transportation consisted of a bicycle for trips to the village and a twenty-year-old van to carry his anvil, his portable forge, and all his farrier tools.

The only other resident of the cottage was a black tomcat with a missing ear, who was only slightly evil. Hugh cherry-picked his clients carefully, preferring to deal with the farm folk who'd lived on these lands for generations, rather than the rich bastards who'd come here from London or Portsmouth or Southampton in hopes of escaping from the global rat race via the liberal application of money.

Hugh drove through the gate leading to Mary Walthorpe's stable yard and backed his van up to the large double doors of the barn, donning his mask to combat the latest pandemic that had been sweeping the globe. Mary was a spry ninety-one years of age. She'd been born on this very farm and lived here all her life, following in her father and grandfather's footsteps of breeding hunting dogs and big, raw-boned foxhunters to follow them over whatever terrain they might encounter.

Mary was one of the few people these days who didn't grate against Hugh's nerves. Everyone was twitchy—and the twitchiness grew worse and worse with the passing of each decade. However, Mary claimed that at her age, she didn't have time for 'the vapors,' as she called it. So, she doddered around, overseeing her sons and grandsons and granddaughters as they ran the stables and the kennels. She still inspected every shoeing job Hugh did personally, and she had a hell of a good eye for it. Also, she wouldn't stand for moldy hay in the barn, a fact

Hugh appreciated even some one hundred years after the advent of phosgene gas warfare.

Hugh greeted her as he stepped out of the van's driver seat. "Morning, luv. How's the family keeping?"

Deep wrinkles creased the corners of Mary's eyes as she gifted him with a distracted smile beneath her mask. "Can't complain, pet. Little Dorrie had a bad turn early last month, but she's bounced back well enough. And you?"

"Can't complain," Hugh echoed.

"Any plans for Easter?" Mary asked.

Hugh covered an involuntary wince. "Oh, you know. The usual," he managed, painfully aware that he was unlikely to be seeing Morpheus for their normal centenary meeting. "I imagine you'll have a full house to feed?"

Mary laughed. "Oh, yes. My brother and his family are coming over from Dorset, assuming his wife is well enough to travel—but I don't want to keep you here with idle chitchat, dear. I know you've got a full schedule." She turned to look over her shoulder with a frown, unhooking her mask from one ear. "Oy, George!" she bellowed. "Get Falcon up here! It's rude to keep the blacksmith waiting!"

"He's down in his stall, Ma!" came the answering shout from the far end of the barn.

Concerned, Hugh followed Mary toward the source of the voice. Indeed, a handsome bay gelding wearing a stable rug lay on its side amongst the deeply bedded straw of the stall. The animal's eyes moved rapidly beneath its eyelids, its legs held out straight and trembling. At intervals, its muscles jerked hard, like a palsy victim.

"Dreaming," Mary said sadly.

Hugh watched with a heavy heart as the horse's mouth opened in a silent scream.

"Should I wake 'im?" asked George.

"No," Mary said. "He'll be less frightened if you leave him to wake up naturally. Get Buttercup instead, we'll shoe her first."

George nodded and went to retrieve the horse a few stalls down.

"You're too young to remember it," Mary murmured to Hugh, "but back in the old days, they dreamed of galloping and playing. Nice things. You could watch their legs making the motions. Sometimes you could even see them clearing imaginary jumps. Same with the dogs—they'd chase rabbits while they slept."

"My grandfather used to talk about that," Hugh lied. He remembered those kinder times all too well—probably far better than Mary, who would have been a child when things first began to change.

"No one likes to talk about it now," Mary said wistfully. "I think it was something that happened during the war, though. World War II, I mean. Some kind of secret weapon that neither side would admit to."

On his worst days, Hugh worried that the collapse of dreams was somehow his fault. He'd angered the god responsible for overseeing such things, and in the fickle way of gods, Morpheus had withdrawn his gifts from the whole of the Earth in retribution.

On his less bad days, Hugh was terrified that something else had happened to prevent Morpheus from carrying out his duties. And when those thoughts came, Hugh pulled out the oldest brandy he owned and swilled it until he was too drunk to focus on his itching need to *know*.

Mary sighed, still watching the gelding twitch and jerk. "He'll wake up soon enough." She sounded as though she were reassuring herself, not Hugh. "And in the meantime, here's Buttercup. I want to move the breakover point of her front hooves back a bit. She's been clipping them with her hind hooves at the trot when she's coming due for a trim."

Hugh pulled his focus away from things he couldn't change, examining the stride of the rangy chestnut mare as George walked her down the barn aisle. "Yes, I see what you mean. You have a keen eye, Mary. I've got some new horseshoes with a rolled toe that might be just the thing for her. Here, let me show you."

In her current circumstances, Iridaceae had been hard pressed to keep track of the passage of time in the Sublunary. No one in the Night Lands wanted to talk to an owl—at least, not beyond snapping at her to *'go away'* and *'stop dumping wine in my lap.'*

Eventually, she'd given up seeking outside help and installed herself in Morpheus' throne room with its cloudy mirrors covering every wall. Owls were, if nothing else, sharp-eyed. The mirrors mostly showed a mass of swirling confusion that reflected the absence of a controlling force to guide the oneiri in their duties. Nevertheless, a patient observer could occasionally catch a glimpse of something useful.

Morpheus had ensured that she was fluent in reading and writing several of the major human languages, so a glimpse of a newspaper's front page, or a calendar surfacing for a moment amidst the swirl of unfocused dreams, was enough to give her an idea of the current date in the mortal realm.

It had taken much longer, but eventually she'd also run across the dreams of the one human she desperately needed to see. At first, it was merely a fleeting connection, found and quickly lost. But as she spent day after lonely day ensconced among the mirrors, she was able to get a better feel for finding him.

And so it had gone, as first years, then decades passed in the Sublunary.

Iridaceae was not a god. Far from it. But even without her master's presence, she did not age within the Night Lands. Such was the gift of the realm of immortals, even to one such as her.

Now, the time for action was fast approaching. Still, she was as stuck as ever, unable to either shift form or travel between the realms on her own.

There were few things she wanted to do less than abase herself before Morpheus' self-absorbed prat of a younger brother. And yet… it was either Phantasos or Thanatus. Iridaceae had a sneaking suspicion that the God of Death was as likely to toss her into the realm of Tartarus as accept her into his service.

That was how she found herself bringing the God of Fantasy the shiniest baubles she could find among Morpheus' abandoned treasure trove of dream-things.

Sapphires.

Emeralds.

Pearls.

Opals that seemed to burn with an inner fire.

Exquisitely carved ostrich eggs.

Gold jewelry.

She dropped every offered gift at Phantasos' feet before bowing low, ducking her head and covering it with the sweep of a wing as though she could not bear to look upon his beauty.

At first, he chased her off. Gradually, curiosity overcame his irritation with her. Until finally, one day, he crossed his arms and looked down at her in consternation.

"Are you seeking a new master, bird?"

Iridaceae lowered her wing and bobbed her head up and down in enthusiastic agreement, while trying not to regurgitate the mouse she'd eaten earlier out of pure disgust.

"*Hmph*," Phantasos said with a haughty sniff. "Well, I suppose it might be amusing, if nothing else."

With a languid gesture of one manicured hand, he sent a wave of power into her. For the first time in decades, her body twisted and morphed into its human shape. She resisted the urge to squawk in surprise.

Phantasos raised a graceful eyebrow. "This means you're my servant now, little bird. You'll obey my orders, or I'll toss you out on your feathered ear."

Iridaceae swept into another bow, her limbs feeling long and clumsy after so long without practice. "Of course, my lord. Consider me at your command."

———————◆———————

Meanwhile, in a forgotten underground bunker, an emaciated figure crouched in the darkness—unmoving and unseeing.

Alone.

Covered from head to foot in gray dust, the figure might have been a stone statue representing the depths of defeat and misery... except for the ancient tear tracks spidering down the gaunt planes of its cheeks.

TWENTY-TWO

2021 A.D.

IRIDACEAE WAS, AS IT turned out, rather good at being a spy. It wasn't something she'd ever tried her hand at before, but it utilized skills she'd honed while hunting — stealth, observation, and picking her moment.

This hitherto unexplored talent ended up becoming extremely useful in her efforts to curry favor with her new — *temporary* — master. Phantasos was delighted to gain access to gossip and intrigue in the Night Lands before anyone else did. And Iridaceae was happy enough to keep his newfound addiction fed if it got her what she wanted.

It didn't hurt that some of this gossip and intrigue might end up being relevant to her own unstated goals. She'd learned, for instance, that Thanatus had caught Phobetor seducing some of the darker oneiri away from Morpheus' domain and into his own. Thanatus had apparently decided not to take any action on the matter after Phobetor assured him that the gambit would ultimately provide him with more mortal souls to reap in the Sublunary.

Iridaceae had barely managed to stifle a hoot of outrage when she'd overheard two of the remaining oneiri discussing the matter. She already knew that the creatures weren't inherently loyal, but the idea that any of them would turn to *Phobetor*, of all the gods, made her blood boil.

She harbored suspicions of her own about the God of Fear. But while she had learned many interesting things, she had no direct proof that he'd been involved with Morpheus' ill-fated visit to the human realm in 1940 A.D.

With few other choices, she dutifully relayed everything she learned to Phantasos, and in return, he began to soften toward her. Meanwhile, she kept a close eye on the upcoming date of the humans' spring holy day.

While it was not imperative that her visit to the Sublunary take place on that day, it would certainly simplify matters. For one thing, it was a near certainty that Hugh de Ferrers would be thinking about Morpheus and his realm during the night before *Easter*, and that would make finding his mirror among the confusion of the collective unconscious easier.

<hr>

"My Lord?" Iridaceae bowed low before Phantasos' extravagant throne, having just finished delivering the latest round of scandalous gossip. "There is one more thing, if I may."

"Yes, little bird," the god of fantasy said. "What is it? You've done well in your efforts, yet again."

"I have a request," she said humbly. "It is but a small thing, yet it eats at me."

Phantasos waved a disinterested hand in her direction. "Well, go on then. Make your appeal."

She chanced a look at him from beneath her lashes. "It is... a loose thread, I suppose you might say. My former master had a particular human that he visited every hundred years on a certain day. That day is tomorrow."

Phantasos frowned, his haughty brow furrowing. "Every hundred years? Impossible. They barely live for a single century. Less, usually."

Iridaceae bowed lower. "This human is immortal. The result of a wager between your brother and Thanatus, as I understand it. I feel it would be a kindness to visit him and inform him that Morpheus will not be attending any future meetings. Otherwise, he may worry."

Phantasos made a scoffing noise. "*Pfft*. Why should I care if a human worries for my absent sibling? If his meeting with this... *person*... was of such concern to him, perhaps he should not have abandoned his duties and disappeared."

Iridaceae gritted her teeth so hard it made her gums hurt.

Forcing calm, she unclenched her jaw and said, "No doubt you are correct, my lord. However, I thought you might find some amusement in it. One might almost say your brother had cultivated a *friendship* with this simple creature. That is rather unusual for a denizen of the Night Lands, is it not?"

She snuck another look at him through her lashes and was gratified to see a spark of interest in his eyes.

"Hmm. A friendship, you say?" His tone made it clear that she had piqued his curiosity, if only to investigate something that might paint his missing brother in a poor light.

"Indeed so, my lord," she confirmed. "In fact, Morpheus had been known to..." She lowered her voice conspiratorially. "... *interfere* on this human's behalf."

Unholy glee lit the god's face. "*Really*? My stick-up-the-arse brother broke a *rule*?" He let out a startled laugh. "This I must see. Very well, little bird. I will grant your request. There's only one problem. How do you expect me to find this random human? I'm not the one who gave him immortality."

Iridaceae spoke quickly, before he could suggest approaching Thanatus for help. "I can find him in the mirrors within Morpheus' palace. He will be anticipating the visit; it shouldn't be difficult."

"It had better not be," Phantasos said. "I'm willing to indulge you, but not if it's going to be *bothersome*."

"I'm certain it won't be," Iridaceae assured him, hoping it was true. "If it pleases you, I will go ahead to your brother's throne room and seek out the connection."

"You do that." He made a shooing motion.

"Thank you, my lord. You are truly a benevolent master." She rose to her feet and hurried toward the exit.

"*Hmph*. Friends with a human..." The words followed her out, rife with speculation.

Too impatient to rely on her feet, Iridaceae transformed into an owl and flew as fast as she could to the vast room of mirrors before transforming back to human form. Panic fluttered in her chest as she searched the ever-shifting images for a flash of familiarity.

She was still looking when Phantasos strode in.

"Well?" he demanded.

In desperation, she ran her gaze more quickly over the hazy reflective surfaces. A flash of dark, thistledown hair and the glint of a stormy blue eye caught her attention. "There!" she cried, pointing to the image of her true master even as a pang stabbed at her heart.

"I see," Phantasos said, tilting his head as he examined the strangely flattering, rose-tinted memory of a hawk-sharp face.

Iridaceae took a moment to be thankful for the fact that the image of Morpheus was neither naked nor lying debauched in a bed.

Small mercies.

"May we go?" she asked. "Dreams these days are fleeting… and often unpleasant."

"Only because my brother abandoned his post," Phantasos snapped, abruptly peevish. After a moment, he subsided with a sigh. "Yes, let's go. Come along, little bird."

Phantasos took her arm, not bothering to fashion clothing for her to wear. Even though Iridaceae was no great aficionado of clothes, the oversight still rankled. It didn't matter, though. All that mattered was reaching someone who might care that her master had been captured. That he had been *hurt.*

The palace faded away, replaced with a modest bedroom barely tinged gray by the predawn light filtering through a curtained window. A black cat yowled its startlement at their sudden appearance, launching itself from the bed and disappearing through the door.

180

The human figure beneath the covers stirred, mumbled something, and abruptly lurched bolt upright with a gasp. A hand fumbled clumsily for the lamp on a table next to the bed, and a moment later, a circle of yellow light illuminated Hugh de Ferrers, Iridaceae, and Phantasos as three points of a very awkward triangle.

De Ferrers was dressed in a thin cotton shirt and had dark circles under his eyes. He was also gaping at them like a startled fish. His gaze darted back and forth between Iridaceae's nakedness and the embodiment of mortal fantasy.

Eventually, his jaw snapped shut. "You came," he said slowly. "I didn't think you would."

Iridaceae frowned in confusion and looked over at her companion. Where a beautiful young man with golden curls had stood a moment before, there now stood a noticeably idealized version of Morpheus.

The vision of Morpheus frowned as well, looking down at his hands for a beat before lifting them to poke at the sharp planes of his face and touch his wild black hair.

Then, Phantasos began to laugh. "Oh," he cackled. "Oh, dear me. I do believe you're in for a shock, immortal or no. My, my — you *do* have it bad for him, don't you? I almost feel sorry for you."

With that, his features shifted back to their usual appearance — beautiful and haughty, a perfect, untouchable object of human desire.

Except, apparently, for one Hugh de Ferrers, who blinked at both of them before plaintively demanding, "Erm. Excuse me, but could someone please tell me what the *ever-loving fuck* is going on?"

TWENTY-THREE

2021 A.D.

IRIDACEAE LEANED forward, her hands itching to grab de Ferrers by the shirt front and shake him until his teeth rattled in her desperation to *make someone listen.*

"Morpheus is missing," she said, speaking quickly. "He needs help! He was hurt… the humans tricked him into coming here and I think they captured him somehow —"

De Ferrers' eyes widened in alarm, but a rough hand grabbed Iridaceae by the arm and whipped her around.

"Impudent creature!" Phantasos hissed. "Do you desire to play me for a fool? How dare you attempt to deceive me in such a way!" He sent a wave of power through her like a slap across the face, releasing her as her body twisted and shrank, returning to the form of an owl. "Stay here and *rot,* you feathered beast. You are no servant of mine!"

She shrieked with frustration and flew at his face, talons outstretched — but he was already gone. In her rage, she flew through the place where he'd just been and nearly collided with a bookshelf set against the far wall.

"Iridaceae!" De Ferrers had managed to fight his way free of the twisted bedclothes and stagger to his feet.

She flapped awkwardly through a tight turn in the small room, nearly taking out the lamp as she returned to him. Furious and distraught, she landed on his arm and clambered up to perch on his shoulder. She knew she was probably piercing his skin with her talons, but all she could do was turn her head and hide her face against his hair, beside herself with the need for some kind of comfort.

There was no way the human would be able to help her based on such a paltry amount of information. And now she was trapped in the human realm, once more without a voice. If she could have wept in this form, she would have done it.

She had failed her master, and the knowledge scalded her heart like acid.

—◆—

Hugh froze as the frantic owl flew at him, flapping to a neat landing on the arm he'd raised instinctively to protect his face. Iridaceae's razor-sharp claws bloodied him as she hopped up the length of his bicep to perch on his shoulder, but all she did once she'd gained a secure roost there was to nestle her feathered head against the crook of his neck and shake.

It felt, for all the world, like a child rushing into a protector's embrace for solace. Hesitantly, Hugh lifted his hand and stroked her downy nape, not sure if he was about to get pecked in the eye for his troubles.

Iridaceae's small body trembled, hunching inward as though she could make herself smaller still.

Hugh made a valiant effort to shake the cobwebs of interrupted sleep from his mind and think logically. Or... as logically as one *could* think, when confronted with a hysterical shape-shifting owl and the vision of his oldest friend, who'd then transformed into a male fashion model and patronized him for a bit before getting angry and storming off.

On reflection, it would probably be fair to show himself a bit of leniency for not immediately having his shit together. But Iridaceae's words before the runway model had grabbed her still rang in his ears like a bell.

Morpheus missing. Hurt. Possibly captured.

What could hurt a god, much less take one captive? Unbidden, Hugh thought about the collapse of dreams... the world's slow slide into insanity. Had he dreamed earlier tonight? If so, he didn't remember it. These days, that was usually a mercy.

Then there was the question of his unthinking reaction to the news. He'd sent Morpheus away a century ago. They'd exchanged angry words—bad enough that Hugh had spent much of the last hundred years under the assumption that he would never see his inhuman benefactor again. And yet, at the first suggestion of Morpheus being in danger, here he was, ready to leap into action and do... what, exactly?

He sighed, setting his own conflicted reactions aside in favor of dealing with Iridaceae. He stroked her soft feathers again before tapping her very lightly on the back of her skull with a fingertip. "Hey. I know you're upset, but I need more details. Can you speak when you're in this form?"

She did at least lift her head, but the low hoot she emitted very clearly conveyed, *do I look like I can speak, you blithering idiot?*

Which… fair enough.

"All right," he said, and carefully transferred her from his shoulder onto the back of a handy wooden chair. "Can you bob your head up and down for yes, and move it side to side for no?"

A slight hesitation, and she bobbed her head.

"Terrific," he told her, not feeling remotely prepared to play the world's strangest game of twenty questions this early in the morning. "You said Morpheus was hurt. Were you with him? Did you see it happen?"

Another head-bob.

"And you think he was captured. Are you sure about that?"

A longer hesitation, followed by a negative shake.

"You haven't seen him since, though?"

A negative headshake.

"Did this happen recently?" He could guess the answer to that one, unfortunately, based on the slow transformation of the world's dreams.

Another negative shake. *Fuck.* That was definitely something he hadn't wanted to be right about.

So, it had to be after 1921, when he'd last seen Morpheus in person.

"Before 1950?" he asked, hoping to narrow it down decade by decade.

But Iridaceae only blinked golden eyes at him. His stomach sank.

"Do you know what year it was?"

A positive nod. Then she immediately dipped her head, as though embarrassed by her inability to communicate efficiently.

This wasn't going to work. He needed more information fast, and this wasn't the way to get it.

"All right. I understand that you can't speak when you're an owl," he said, "but do you know how to read and write English? Or French, Dutch, or Spanish, in a pinch?"

She bobbed her head yes, then cocked it at an angle like a confused dog.

"Well, then—this approach is likely to bring its own set of frustrations, but I have an idea. Come with me?" He rummaged in a drawer for another shirt, which he wrapped around his forearm, covering the trail of scratches and punctures that were already starting to scab over.

Iridaceae hopped onto the makeshift gauntlet and let him carry her into the cozy sitting room, where he had an old wooden desk set up in one corner. On it sat a vintage IBM Selectric electronic typewriter—his answer to the ubiquitous computers that everyone seemed to favor these days. He could use it to type up invoices for his clients, or letters to his solicitors, or his fiftieth attempt at finishing a novel whenever he reached a level of such monumental boredom that trying to write a book once again seemed like a good idea.

And, just perhaps, he could use it to interrogate a sentient, shape-shifting owl who had apparently been the last person to see Morpheus before he disappeared under mysterious circumstances. He set Iridaceae on the back of his well-used desk chair and pointed at the typewriter.

"Do you know what this is?" he asked.

A negative headshake.

"This is a machine for writing things down without using a pen or pencil." He slid a piece of paper into the slot behind the typewriter's platen and hit the index key repeatedly until it rolled forward into the typing area. "You hit the key for the letter you want, and the machine transfers that letter onto the paper. See?"

She watched avidly as he demonstrated, typing *'Can you peck the letters with your beak to write?'*

When he was done, she tilted her head again, large eyes darting from the keyboard to the paper and back again. She hopped onto the edge of the desk, gripping it with her talons. Hugh carefully slid the Selectric closer to her.

She leaned forward and pecked at the machine. Once… twice… three times.

When she straightened, the paper read *'yws.'*

"Brilliant," he said. "Now, take your time and tell me what happened."

Iridaceae fluttered her wings for a moment before settling down and starting to type, one painstaking letter at a time.

TWENTY-FOUR

2021 A.D

TERRIBLE SPELLING had never been quite so alarming before. Hugh read over the barely intelligible page one more time, forcing his brain to work around the dearth of spaces, punctuation, and paragraph breaks to make sure he'd noted all the relevant points.

Thirteen dreaming humans in military uniforms appearing every night in Morpheus' throne room, standing around him in a circle and staring at him, fingers pointing accusingly. Morpheus' eventual decision to follow one of them back to the waking realm, in an attempt to discover the meaning behind this odd and frankly rather disconcerting behavior.

An echoing concrete bunker. A circle of thirteen metal cots containing the same dreamers, strapped down and trailing wires from metal bands around their heads. Other humans awake and aware, pointing firearms at them. A shout, an explosion of noise.

Blood.

If Morpheus was a god, there shouldn't have been blood. A chill had settled over Hugh's heart upon reading that part for the first time, and it still hadn't abated.

He was trying manfully—and without much success—to ignore the bit about *throne rooms* and *realms*. Morpheus was a deity, so Hugh supposed having a kingdom and a palace, or at least a really impressive temple, was part and parcel. That didn't mean he wasn't planning on having a nice, quiet gibber about it in a private corner someplace later on.

He dragged his focus back to the typewritten page—*then he yelled at mee to go flie and i did adn he shovd me back to the night lands with his powr but aftrward he never came home and no 1 woud listen to me i tried i tried i tried.*

His heart went out to the prickly, eccentric owl who was sometimes a human girl. He set the paper down carefully and turned to her. She was pacing restlessly from side to side on the back of the chair, as though she couldn't stand to be still.

"I'm listening to you now," he said quietly.

That stopped her pacing. She gave a sharp head-to-toe shake, resettling her feathers, and bobbed her head.

Hugh wasn't sure what it said about him that after one badly typed page of text, he was ready to drop his entire life and plunge into some sort of ill-defined investigation-slash-rescue-mission for a man... for a *being*... with whom he'd parted ways a century ago, under conditions of bitter acrimony.

He sighed. "Right. I have questions. That arsehole you came here with. That wasn't Timor... I mean Phobetor. Was it?"

Iridaceae shook her head side to side.

"Another god, then?"

An affirmative nod.

"Another brother?"

A second nod.

Hugh wasn't at all sure he wanted an answer to this part, but... "Why the hell did he look like Morpheus when he first arrived?"

Iridaceae gave the typewriter a meaningful look. Hugh blinked, and quickly placed a new sheet of paper in it for her.

It was a frustrating and extremely literal twist on hunt-and-peck typing, but Hugh waited with barely contained impatience until she straightened, having typed *'god of fantasy'* on the blank page. Hugh let that sink in for precisely one second, at which point blood rushed to his cheeks, heating his face until he was sure it must be bright red.

"Great," he said. "Fab. No, really, that's fab. So, I'm guessing he's no help to us?"

Iridaceae shook her head.

"At least he got you here, the twat." He tried once more to take stock of the situation. "Next question. This concrete bunker. Could you find it again? On a map, or even by leading me there?"

She ducked her head and gave him a negative shake. *Only saw insde*, she typed. *Came strait frm night lands.*

His heart sank.

From the context, he gathered the Night Lands were Morpheus' home… perhaps all of the gods'. It would make sense if that's where he went when he suddenly appeared from nowhere or disappeared without a trace. Morpheus had sent Iridaceae there when danger threatened, and apparently it had taken her this long to get back to the real world.

Which brought them to the next question. "Do you know what year this happened? What date?"

Iridaceae flapped her wings excitedly and leaned down to peck the keyboard.

1-9-4-0.

192

Hugh's breath caught. Nausea roiled in his gut. "He's been missing for *eighty years*?"

The owl blinked at him.

He tried to remember roughly what he'd been doing in 1940. That had been the year when things in Western Europe went to hell in a handbasket. He'd spent the first part of the year involved in the evacuation of at-risk children from Eastern Europe to Britain, and the second half hiding away in French slums, engaging in sabotage and espionage against the invading Germans.

And not long after he'd arrived in Paris…

Oh.

Oh.

"I had a nightmare," he said blankly, before recalling himself to his wide-eyed audience of one. "In 1940. It was the first one I'd had since the war started. I thought he'd finally had enough of coddling me after we fought in 1921."

Iridaceae stared at him, her thoughts unreadable inside her feathered skull.

Hugh lifted a hand to his temple, as though he could physically pull the memory to the forefront. "It must have been… late July? No, August. It was in early August. The Germans hadn't started bombing London yet, but they were hitting ships in the Channel and sending night raids against the harbors."

He'd never wished for a set of diaries more than he did in that moment. But he hadn't really been in the habit of keeping them, and even if he had been, it wouldn't have been practical during that particular period of his stupidly long life.

He let his hand fall. "Okay. So, we've got a time frame of a couple of weeks in 1940, and a description of the inside of the facility where you two were attacked, but not a map location. You said the dreamers were wearing uniforms, so it must have been a military operation of some kind."

Iridaceae nodded rapidly.

"There were all sorts of whispers that Hitler and his top advisors were obsessed with the occult," he went on. "Is it possible he managed to successfully trap a god? Christ, that sounds insane..."

But Iridaceae was shaking her head. She hopped forward and started typing again. *Not germn. Talkd liek you.*

Hugh looked at the words for a long moment before his brain rebooted and the sense of them untangled itself.

"They were English?" He paused. "You don't mean American, do you?" Surely Britain wouldn't have been dabbling in that kind of supernatural crap. It was impossible to picture his own countrymen dealing in magic and hooking men up to machines to make them dream in tandem. They were far too earthbound for something like that.

Weren't they?

She shook her head again and typed '*liek u*' next to the previous passage for emphasis. His instinct was to dismiss the idea as preposterous, but there'd been no hesitation in Iridaceae's response. Surely, she must be exposed to all sorts of accents as the companion of the god of dreams and nightmares. If she said they were English and not American or Australian or Canadian, they probably were.

On the positive side, he was already in England. If that was the scene of this eighty-year-old crime, it would at least make it simpler to start investigating. He firmly refused to think about how many times someone could have been moved over the course of eight decades, or whether it was possible for a god to die.

"Here's the plan," he said instead. "I'm going to renew some old acquaintances. If the British military was keeping a god captive in a bunker somewhere during the Blitz, there should be whispers about it in the paranormal research community."

Unfortunately, most of those 'old acquaintances' were old enough that he'd have to pose as his own son, or a great nephew or something. It was quite possible he'd end up having to abandon his current life if he got too deep into this, or risk drawing unwanted attention to himself.

Again, it occurred to him that what he was doing probably wasn't normal behavior when it came to helping a bloke who'd cheerfully ditched him a century ago. Mind you, the same bloke had continued to watch over him as he slept until, apparently, he couldn't do so anymore.

Hugh was no more capable of shrugging and consigning Morpheus to his unknown fate than he was of sprouting wings and taking flight. Speaking of which…

"Do you need anything, Iridaceae? What do owls eat, anyway?"

Could you buy owl kibble at the pet store?

Iridaceae started typing again. *U live in woods.*

Ah. Right.

"Good point. I'll open a window for you." Mentally, he started compiling a list of people to contact. "Fuck, I'm probably going to have to break down and buy a laptop. Everyone uses email these days."

Iridaceae gave a winged shrug of agreement and hopped onto the windowsill as he opened the casement for her. A moment later, she'd disappeared into the murky predawn—leaving Hugh wondering vaguely how much of what had just happened had been real.

He sighed and went to figure out how to use the internet on his mobile phone.

TWENTY-FIVE

2021 A.D.

"I STILL HATE this thing," Hugh muttered, scrolling his fingertips along the trackpad of the shiny silver laptop he'd been forced to buy two months ago. His cat watched the proceedings warily from his perch on the back of the old davenport across the room.

Iridaceae fluttered her wings in a shooing motion to get Hugh out of her way before leaning down and pecking *'easier to type tho'* into the text window he'd left open for her. Living with a sentient owl wasn't something Hugh had anticipated being on his twenty-first century bingo card—but on the positive side, between Iridaceae and Baphometh, there wasn't a mouse or a shrew to be found anywhere within one hundred meters of the cottage these days.

He elbowed his way back into scrolling position and resumed his slog through the morning's email. "I don't like spam from a can, and I don't like it in my bloody inbox, either. How did these people even get my address?"

Iridaceae gave an avian shrug and hopped onto his shoulder to snoop in his messages.

The evening after her arrival with Morpheus' prancing ponce of a brother, Hugh had reluctantly dragged himself into the internet age and started looking up old acquaintances from the nineteen sixties. *Old* being the operative word, since more than fifty years had passed in the interim. Some of them were still alive and had kept up with the times, at least to the extent of maintaining email addresses and social media accounts. One even had her own website related to paranormal phenomena.

While most of the country had been busy smoking weed and standing around in muddy fields listening to rock music, Hugh had been going through an occultist phase. He'd never quite got up the courage to try magic for himself — the memory of a witch-hunting mob pounding down your door had a way of sticking with a person. Still, he'd developed quite a little network of people who didn't suffer from the same hang-ups as he did.

As far as he could tell, most of them had been utter, bollocking frauds. And most of them were dead, anyway… or at least, not easily searchable online. Then, there was the added complication of having to approach them in the guise of being his own great nephew. His first dozen attempts at reaching out hadn't yielded a single response, probably because he hadn't been all that memorable in his guise as Henry de Ferrers.

Occupational hazard — if he'd learned one thing in his eight centuries of life, it was that being *memorable* was to be avoided at all costs.

It was the public contact page on Philomena's ridiculous conspiracy website that finally gave him his first hit. She'd replied, telling him that she remembered Hugh from when he'd been Henry, that she still lived in London, and of *course* she'd love to meet with him to catch up on old times over tea.

It wasn't much, but it was a start.

"Goodness, look at you!" she'd said upon opening the door to him. "You really are the spitting image of him, even wearing that silly plague mask. Come in, come in!"

It quickly became apparent that public masking mandates were one of Philomena's pet conspiracy theories. She wasn't wearing one and obviously didn't intend to. Hugh eventually agreed to a socially distanced cup of tea outside on the terrace as a reluctant compromise.

"Now," she'd asked once they were settled, "what brings you to my door? I haven't thought of dear old Henry for such a long time. Poor bloke — he was so fascinated by it all, but there wasn't a magical bone in his body!"

The irony of someone saying that to a man who'd lived more than eight hundred years hung in the air like smoke signals. Hugh swallowed the impulse to point out that there wasn't a magical bone in *her* body, either... despite what she always claimed to anyone willing to listen.

"So, I have this idea," he said instead, "about whatever it was that happened to dreams during the Second World War. I'd love your insights on how I might seek evidence to support my hypothesis." And then he'd gone on to outline the fantastical notion of the British military dabbling in the occult — an attempt to counter Hitler's alleged research into supernatural weapons.

She'd gobbled up the crazy-sounding theory with a spoon, her muddy brown eyes growing brighter and brighter with excitement as he spoke. After which, she'd given an excited wriggle in her seat and told him to leave everything to her, because this was going to be *brilliant*.

That enthusiastic directive hadn't yielded much of anything useful during the following weeks, so Hugh had kept himself busy trying to find other ways to plug in to whatever passed for the current occult elite of modern Britain. Unfortunately, they were a tight-knit lot—just as they always had been. They'd learned long ago that insularity was a defense mechanism against an unkind press seeking to portray them as a bunch of eccentric whack-jobs.

Mind you, in Hugh's experience, they *were* a bunch of eccentric whack jobs.

But today, at the very bottom of his seemingly endless queue of unread emails, sat a new message from Philomena. *'Someone you'll want to meet'* read the subject line. Hugh tried not to get his hopes up as he opened it.

Dear Hugh,

I've just made the acquaintance of the most charming young woman, thanks to a colleague who keeps an eye on the magical artifact market. Her grandfather was in the army during the War, and he bequeathed her a terribly interesting item, along with an equally interesting story. I should love to put the two of you in touch.

Yours,

Philomena Waldenpole

Hugh drew in a sharp breath before he could catch himself. Iridaceae gave an excited hoot and shook her small body, her soft feathers brushing against Hugh's ear.

"We need to keep our expectations moderated," Hugh warned, not sure if it was for Iridaceae's benefit or his own. The sentiment was belied by the way his heart pounded in excitement within his chest. "This could be totally unrelated, or it could be a load of old rot. Most paranormal stuff is, from what I've seen."

Iridaceae, unfazed, launched herself from his shoulder and flew excitedly around the room, nearly toppling an antique vase from the top of a bookshelf. Hugh tried not to let his thoughts fly off in a similar manner as he typed out a reply, offering to meet with the young woman as soon as possible.

———◆———

The woman in question was in her mid-twenties, at a guess. She had the look of someone who slept both seldom and poorly, as though she were one of the unlucky ones who suffered the most from disordered dreaming. Her hair was red, her complexion was pale, and her hazel eyes were bloodshot.

She arrived for their appointment in a pleasant little café in the company of Philomena, who waved cheerfully upon sighting Hugh at his table in the back corner.

"Here we are, my dears," she greeted, herding her charge toward a seat across from him like a broody hen with one chick. "Introductions are in order, I believe. Hugh, this is Deirdre Johnson, the girl I told you about. Deirdre, this is Hugh de Ferrers, the great nephew of a dear old friend of mine from many years ago."

Hugh stifled a snort, wondering when '*dear old Henry*' had graduated from being a casual acquaintance to a bosom friend. He rose, stretching out a hand to shake Deirdre's. Her grip was delicate, almost limp, but she mustered a nervous smile for him.

"Good to meet you Deirdre," he said, returning to his seat once she and Philomena had settled themselves. "I appreciate your willingness to talk to me."

"It's no trouble," Deirdre said. There was an eager, almost desperate timbre to her light voice. "Honestly, it's kind of a relief to find people who don't think I'm crazy."

Hugh summoned his most reassuring smile; the one he used for horse owners who were convinced their precious mounts would never be sound again after pulling up with a bruised sole or a hoof abscess. "Not to worry. We're all a bit crazy here. Philomena tells me you've come into possession of an unusual artifact from the Second World War? Could you tell me about it?"

"I can do better than that," Deirdre said, her voice turning grim. "So, the short version is that my grandfather served in the war. Just before the Germans started bombing London, he was attached to the intelligence branch as a corporal. After the enemy destroyed a top-secret facility in a bombing run, he was part of the crew sent in to clean up."

Hugh frowned. "If he was telling other people things like that, he was asking for trouble under the Official Secrets Act, wasn't he?"

Deirdre shrugged. "He was on his death bed, so I don't think he really cared very much by that point, you know? Anyway, he was part of a team sent to look for survivors in this secret underground bunker. There weren't any. Or rather, there was only one. He called it a creature, but he also said it looked like a man."

Philomena caught Hugh's eye, offering him a significant quirk of one silver eyebrow. Hugh held himself very still in an effort not to vault across the table like a madman and shake the rest of the story out of the poor woman. "Oh?"

Deirdre nodded. "He said it was kept chained, and that his commanding officer ordered them to leave it behind. After they retrieved all of the dead soldiers they could find, they blasted the entrance of the bunker to seal it. Afterward, they were told never to speak about what they'd seen inside."

Hugh could feel his hands trembling with suppressed excitement. He clasped them on his lap, out of view beneath the table. "And this artifact he gave you?"

"He willed it to me when he passed," she said. "Maybe because I was the only one who would listen to his stories without discounting them. My parents thought he was addled… just making things up."

She rummaged in the inner pocket of her jacket and came up with something small enclosed in her hand. "He said he picked this up from the floor of the bunker when no one else was looking. Told me it was the key to unleash a demon so powerful that the War Office thought they could use it to turn the tides of the war."

Turning her hand palm up, she uncurled her fingers to reveal a glowing metal key.

TWENTY-SIX

2021 A.D.

IT TOOK EVERY bit of control Hugh possessed not to grab for the shining golden key cradled in the young woman's hand. "Huh," he managed. "And he said this creature was chained up? So, this is the actual key to unlock those chains?"

"He certainly believed so," Deirdre said, closing her fingers around the key again.

Hugh couldn't prevent a small twitch as it disappeared from view. "That's fascinating. I don't suppose he told you the location of this secret bunker as well?"

Deirdre nodded. "He did. He said he always intended to go back and try to take the demon's power for himself, but as far as I know, he never followed through. I think he was too frightened of it."

Smart bloke, Hugh thought.

"What about you?" he asked. "Did you ever go?"

Something in Deirdre's expression twisted for a flicker of a moment before she covered it.

"Once. There's an eight-foot fence topped with razor wire all around the area. The inside just looks like a big, grassy hill."

"Guards?" Hugh asked, aware that he sounded far too keen to successfully come across as an eccentric occultist pursuing a random bit of fanciful nonsense.

She shook her head. "Didn't see any. There's no guard house or anything, just an old dirt track leading up to the locked gate. I turned around and came home. Didn't want to get in trouble if there were cameras around the place, and anyway, the chains looked too thick for bolt cutters."

"Probably wise," he said.

Philomena had been watching the exchange with interest. "I told you I had a friend keeping an eye on the artifact market, yes? Terry called me when he came across a description of the key on an auction site. The listing had been cancelled, but they hadn't removed the information yet."

Deirdre's face screwed up in irritation. "They thought it might be radioactive because of the glow, so they refused to sell it for safety reasons. I told them it wasn't."

"You've checked it?" Hugh asked quickly. Not that there was much radiation could do to him on a permanent basis—just as well with all the terrorist dirty bombs that had been going off in major cities over the past couple of decades. Philomena, on the other hand…

"Course I did," Deirdre said. "Got a Geiger counter and everything. It's magic, not bloody plutonium."

He relaxed marginally. "Good to know. So, you wanted to sell it, but the auction house backed out. Have you considered a private sale?"

Please, please — consider a private sale. I don't want to take that key from you by force, but I'll damned well do it if it comes to that.

"Are you joking? Why else do you think I'm here, mate?" She stared at him like she was worried about his intelligence level.

"Good. That's good," he said. "How much do you want for it?"

Deirdre blinked, clearly startled. That wasn't how you negotiated the price of a one-of-a-kind article of unknown provenance. Hugh could see her silently reshuffling her thoughts.

"One—" she began, only to cut herself off and clear her throat. She squared her shoulders, meeting his eyes defiantly. "Two hundred thousand quid."

"Done," Hugh said instantly. "Assuming that also includes the location of the bunker."

Deirdre's red-rimmed eyes had grown wide as dinner plates, and Philomena was giving Hugh a very intent look over her half-moon glasses.

"Um… yes?" Deirdre said, her voice almost a squeak.

"Perfect," Hugh told her. "We can go to my bank right now, and I'll get you a draft."

She gaped at him like a fish for a couple of seconds, then snapped her jaw shut. "Brilliant," she said hoarsely.

"Well!" Philomena exclaimed, clapping her wrinkled hands together. "Isn't this all *terribly* exciting!"

◆

Transferring ridiculously large sums of money on short notice had been a *lot* easier a hundred years ago. Eventually, they got it done, though Hugh was beginning to worry that the next step would be blood and urine samples, a lie detector test, and possibly an extracted tooth.

Since the entirety of Hugh's van was taken up by farrier tools with the exception of the driver's seat, Philomena offered to drive Deirdre to the bunker site in her ancient MG two-seater, so Hugh could follow behind them.

"I wouldn't miss this for the world," she said cheerfully. "This is the most fun I've had since Thatcher was Prime Minister!"

Hugh worked very hard at suppressing his irritation. Her chirpy enjoyment of what might very well end up being the underground prison-tomb of a being who couldn't die grated on his nerves. Even worse was the niggling question of whether a god actually *could* die, and if so, under what circumstances. For the thousandth time in the last three-and-a-half months, he flashed back to Iridaceae's description of an explosion of noise followed by a spurt of blood.

If you'd asked Hugh, he wouldn't have said gods could bleed, either.

The café where they'd met up had been in Twickenham, in the southwest edge of London's suburban sprawl. Hugh had half-expected them to head for Porton Down, an area notorious for its secret military research. Instead, they drove south toward Leatherhead and beyond, into the Surrey Hills, a largely unspoiled nature area adjacent to well-kept farmland.

Fifty miles. The place was less than *fifty miles from his bloody house*.

They pulled off a scenic road and onto what looked like an unmaintained farm track—except there were no farms this deep in the woods. At several points, Hugh worried for the MG's suspension and ground clearance, but eventually the track evened out and the woods gave way to a grass covered hilltop.

Ahead lay the razor-wire topped fence Deirdre had described, the chain link overgrown with weeds and ivy. Hugh pulled the van to a stop and stepped out, a dull ache taking up residence in his chest. He'd thought, fancifully, that he might be able to feel Morpheus' presence somehow. There was nothing, but whether it was because Hugh was still only human, or because his friend wasn't here, there was no way to know. Idly, he fingered the glowing key now nestled in his pocket.

The women joined him. Deirdre gestured awkwardly at the fence and the sloping, grass-choked earth beyond. "So, anyway, this is it. Doesn't really look like much, I know."

"Nonsense, my dear," said Philomena. "The most extraordinary things are sometimes found in the most unassuming packages."

"I'm going to walk the perimeter," Hugh told them. "The ground looks pretty rough; probably best if you stay here, Philomena."

Philomena chuckled, lifting a foot clad in an impractical leather sandal. "No argument from me. Deirdre can keep me company. I'm sure we'll have a nice chat while you hike through the weeds."

Deidre attempted a smile and a nod of agreement, but her face was waxen in the dull afternoon light.

Hugh set off, crashing through tall grass and brush in search of a broken or fallen section of fence.

Deirdre hadn't been exaggerating about the gate; the padlocks holding it closed had rusted into solidity over the decades, and the chain was so thick it would require specialist equipment to cut.

As a blacksmith, Hugh could do it, if need be, but he'd prefer to get inside for a proper recce before he committed to that. He trudged along the boundary, dodging the occasional scrubby tree or boulder, taking a right turn when the fence did.

The view inside the fence didn't change much. Deirdre had been accurate when she described it as a grassy hill. It was only when he came to an abandoned and half-buried rail line—by virtue of nearly tripping over it—that he gained his first lead regarding the location of the entrance.

The rails disappeared under the fence, and as he walked farther along the fence line, he could make out the slight variation in plant growth where they ran toward the manmade hill. He turned the next corner, and there it was—a grass-covered dip in the hilltop that spoke of the collapse of something beneath it.

"Bulls eye," he murmured, moving to get the best possible view of the former entrance. It wasn't a very good one, but from what he could see, there was no hint of a gap or hole. If the military's intention had been to seal the bunker, they'd succeeded. Nature had reclaimed it during the intervening eighty-odd years, leaving it just a slowly softening scar on the landscape.

He finished his circuit of the fence and returned to the others, brushing grass seeds and brambles off his clothing before checking for the dozenth time that the key was still safely in his pocket.

"Did you find anything?" Philomena asked breathlessly.

"Yes," he said. "I found out that heavy equipment rental is in my immediate future."

Deidre still looked pallid, but at that, her eyes widened. "You're going to break in?"

"My dear Hugh!" Philomena sounded delighted. "It sounds as though you're discussing wanton destruction of government property!"

Hugh tugged a particularly stubborn bramble from the seat of his trousers and tossed it aside. "You bet your sweet arse I am. *Tonight,* if I can get it organized in time."

TWENTY-SEVEN

2021 A.D.

HUGH DID NOT, in fact, manage to organize the untraceable hire of a lorry and backhoe before the close of business that same day. It was the following night before he managed to procure everything he needed, using a backup identity that he held in reserve for emergencies.

As technology grew ever more entwined with day-to-day life, it became more and more expensive to construct false identities from whole cloth. Documents were no longer enough; these days you also had to hire someone to hack government databases. Frankly, the whole thing was a pain in Hugh's arse.

Poor, fictional 'Howard Farrington' would never see the light of day after this debacle. He had emerged from obscurity for a single hour, his first act consisting of signing a rental agreement at a heavy equipment business located more than a hundred miles from the Surrey Hills. His last act would be to return that same heavy equipment by the end of the week, safe and sound and on time. Then, he would disappear forever.

Let the government try to follow *that* thread anywhere useful... assuming they even noticed or cared that one of their fenced-off World War II sites had been desecrated.

Iridaceae perched on his shoulder as Hugh maneuvered the lorry and its flatbed trailer along the winding dirt track in the moonlight. The lorry's headlamps and the trailer's running lights were turned firmly off—even though there were no houses located near the old bunker, he wasn't in a hurry to advertise his presence unnecessarily.

He knew his owl companion was every bit as on edge as he was, so he didn't fuss at her for digging her talons into the shoulder of the ratty old hoodie he was wearing. The drive down from Ipswich, where he'd rented the equipment, had seemed to take forever. He'd stopped at his house to pick Iridaceae up, along with various supplies that seemed like they might be necessary—first aid kit, blankets, bottled water, torches with extra batteries, tools for cutting metal, and anything else that looked potentially useful.

Finally—*finally*—the dirt road flattened out, revealing a familiar grassy hilltop in the pale silver light of the waning half-moon. The locked gates loomed ahead.

Reining in his jittering impatience, Hugh made himself negotiate the fiddly process of getting the lorry turned around so he could drive straight out when the time came to leave. Praying that he wouldn't get the rig stuck in an unseen ditch, he let out a relieved breath when the maneuver was complete.

He turned off the engine and urged Iridaceae onto his forearm as he opened the door.

"Stay clear of the machinery," he warned her. "Maybe go have a shufti around the site while I'm working. It's possible there's an opening big enough for an owl to get in… but be careful, yeah?"

Iridaceae was gone in a flap of wings before he could draw breath to say anything more—an eight-foot security fence posing no barrier to a bird. Hugh sighed and got out, making his way to the trailer to remove the chains holding the backhoe secured.

The night was still and thankfully cloudless, otherwise he'd have had the devil of a time making it up here without lights. Something rustled in the tall grass near the edge of the woods. He paused, but the noise didn't come again… probably a deer or a fox startled by his presence.

It took a good twenty minutes to release all the safety chains and get the ramps down. The backhoe sputtered a couple of times before chugging to life, its caterpillar treads making short work of the trailer ramps.

Hugh had never been so grateful for his stint in the construction industry during the mid-nineteen seventies. While there were more bells and whistles on the dashboard, the basic controls of the backhoe hadn't changed at all in forty-odd years. It didn't take long for his old instincts to come back; his hands and feet remembering how to make the hunk of yellow-painted steel move and turn like an extension of his own body.

The decades-old chain link gates crumpled like tin beneath the assault of the machine's front bucket. Hugh tore them off their hinges and shoved them aside, trundling into the protected area and heading for the far end, where the original entrance had been swallowed by nature after its collapse.

A pale form swooped and glided over the dip in the ground, moving out of the way as he approached. Apparently, Iridaceae hadn't had any luck finding a breach.

No matter. They'd both be inside before long.

He positioned the backhoe as close as he could to the collapsed entrance, lowered the stabilizer legs, extended the rear arm, and tore into the grassy earth with the steel teeth of the smaller rear bucket.

Over the next hour and a half, the pile of dirt and rubble beside the entrance grew. Hugh moved the backhoe deeper into the area he'd cleared, working doggedly until the digger broke through into empty space, sending up a cloud of dust.

Clamping down on his excitement, he carefully widened the gap until it was roughly six feet by six feet. Setting the engine to idle, he hopped down and pulled out a torch. Rubble and collapsed dirt formed a rough ramp leading into darkness. When he played the beam of light farther down, however, the remnants of a concrete staircase appeared as sharp-edged shadows beyond the detritus.

"Now we're talking," Hugh muttered.

Iridaceae glided down and landed on his arm.

"I'll load the backhoe on the trailer and grab the supplies," he told her. "See if you can find anything inside, but for god's sake, watch out for falling rubble and whatever else might be down there. I'll be as quick as I can."

She shoved off his forearm in a flurry of feathers, disappearing into the depths, where her nocturnal predator's vision would be every bit as good as his electric torch.

Hugh hurried into the operator's seat of the backhoe and headed toward the destroyed gate, telling himself firmly that it had been eighty years since Morpheus had been captured, and another half hour wouldn't make much difference in the grand scheme of things. He needed the first aid kit and his other supplies, and he also needed to be able to leave as fast as possible on the crazy chance that Morpheus really was here.

Please, please, don't let this whole thing be a wild goose chase, he thought, as he drove the machine back onto the trailer and started battening it down with record speed. When he'd done the bare minimum to ensure the backhoe wouldn't slide off the flatbed the first time he went around a turn, he grabbed his supplies from the lorry and started jogging back to the entrance.

The unhappy wildlife lurking at the edge of the forest scuffled again, but nothing short of lions returning to the Surrey Hills would have stopped Hugh at this point. He ignored it, running as fast as he dared over the uneven ground, his backpack flopping against his shoulders.

Iridaceae met him at the newly excavated entrance, flapping excitedly. His heart kicked and jolted into a higher gear.

"You found something?" he asked breathlessly.

By way of answer, she launched herself from the pile of rubble and disappeared inside the bunker with a sharp hoot. Hugh resettled his pack and swept the torch beam downward, finding the best path to clamber into the pit until he could reach the remains of the staircase.

By the time he made it, he was covered in loose dirt and concrete dust. Another excited hoot reached him from deeper in the structure, and he picked his way down, avoiding cracked steps and chunks of fallen rubble.

He'd researched World War II bunkers on the internet the previous night, and most of them were cramped, makeshift affairs. There were hundreds of the things scattered across the countryside, designed to hide small deployments of shock troops who could pop out and blow up bridges or rail lines in the event of German troops making it onto British soil.

By contrast, this one was *massive*. Parts of the roof had collapsed, either during the bomb attack or afterward, victim to the ravages of time. His torch beam barely made a dent in the blackness, but the space echoed, vast and long-dead.

Iridaceae's strident call sounded closer this time. Hugh swept the beam in that direction, skirting slabs of concrete large enough to have crushed anyone unlucky enough to be beneath them. They blocked his view, making it impossible to see anything beyond them—forcing him to follow his ears as Iridaceae's excited cries continued.

His torchlight fell on a skeletal hand sticking out from beneath a fallen slab, and his heartbeat stuttered. Adrenaline kicked in his chest. But, no. Iridaceae was still ahead of him, beyond the collapsed roof section. He sidled around the sad human remains, and nearly fell to his knees when his light illuminated a gap in the destruction.

A gray figure knelt on the filthy floor, head bowed, arms outstretched and chained. It might have been a statue, but for Iridaceae perched on its corded shoulder, frantically preening a messy thatch of hair the same color as the drab concrete around them.

Hugh made a choked noise and slid to his knees in front of the pair, unsure what exactly he was seeing. Stories of Greek heroes turned to stone flitted across his overlong memory.

The harsh beam of light threw deep shadows across the figure's gaunt features. Hesitantly, Hugh reached out a hand to touch, his fingers closing around a wiry bicep. The skin was deeply encrusted with the grit of concrete dust, and cold enough to be made of stone. But the flesh gave under his fingers—muscle and sinew, not marble.

A nearly imperceptible shudder ran through the still form. A trickle of dust fell to the floor.

Heart in throat, Hugh moved his hand to cup a high cheekbone, willing the bowed head to lift. His thumb brushed through fine powder, then caught on a ridge that had hardened like cement.

Tear tracks… decades old.

"Morpheus," he rasped, his own eyes burning.

Iridaceae continued to nudge at the bound god with her beak, making a low, chuntering noise Hugh had never heard from her before.

Another, stronger shudder, and the figure under Hugh's hand sucked in a massive, choking breath. The bowed head whipped up. Bloodshot eyes the color of a glacier's depths peeled open. Clumps of dust detached from thick eyelashes, tickling Hugh's thumb as they fell away.

Panic bloomed behind that unfocused blue gaze, and Hugh tried not to let it engulf him as well.

"Easy," he murmured, as Iridaceae fluttered in dismay. "Easy, we've got you… I've got the key to your chains. We'll get you out, just breathe."

Pulling his hand away from that ancient face was one of the hardest things Hugh had ever done. He fumbled in his pocket, his fingers having suddenly decided not to cooperate with his brain. Finally, they closed around the key. He brought it out, playing the torch beam over the shackle circling the nearest delicate wrist.

The chains, too, were covered in dust. He stuck the handle of the torch between his knees to hold it and started brushing the golden manacle with his sleeve. It glowed with the same eerie, inner light as the key. When he'd cleared out the keyhole as best he could, He jammed the key in and tried to turn it. The mechanism resisted, in dire need of oiling, but it gave way to his hard wrench with a grinding click and popped open.

Hugh threw it to the side with an angry snarl, reaching for the shackle circling Morpheus' neck like a collar next.

A bare croak of a whisper stayed his hand. "No… the bullets… get them out of me… *get them out.*"

The newly freed arm curled inward, fingers clenching at a dark patch over his sternum. Hugh's breath caught in his throat like sandpaper. Iridaceae had described bullets… blood. Surely, they couldn't still be lodged inside his body, all this time later…?

"*Cut them out of me!*" It was a plea. A demand.

Hugh fumbled with the key, clutching it tight. "Morpheus. I… I can't dig a bullet out of your chest in a collapsed bunker with only a hand torch for light! I'll hurt you worse—"

Morpheus' fingers scrabbled at the dark stain, which Hugh was appalled to realize was a literal, *actual* hole in his chest.

"I am a god!" he cried, his obvious panic spilling over. "You will obey me! Get them *out!*"

Hugh had the folding knife in his pocket out and was flipping open the blade before his higher brain functions caught up. It fell from his numb fingers to the hard floor with a clink.

"I'll get them out, I promise," he said, covering the clenching hand with his to still it. "Let me get you unchained and out of this terrible place. Somewhere I can at least see properly—"

Light blinded him, and he threw a hand up instinctively to shade his eyes as he whirled around, looking for the source. Iridaceae squawked and flew upward in an explosion of feathers and flapping wings.

Hugh found himself facing another torch beam, its owner standing between him and the entrance. He squinted, feeling around for his own light on the ground where it had fallen. When he raised it to play over the intruder's face, it illuminated red hair and pale skin in the gray darkness.

"D-don't move," Deirdre Johnson stammered. "Or I'll shoot." She held a black semiautomatic pistol braced across her left forearm. Its barrel, held parallel to her torch, never wavered.

TWENTY-EIGHT

2021 A.D.

THE ABRUPT INCURSION of light and sound into Morpheus' prison beat against his senses like the lashes of a whip.

As a god, he did not dream, nor did he sleep—otherwise he would have thought Hugh and Iridaceae's appearance a flight of fancy, or worried that he had somehow slipped into his brother Phantasos' realm of hallucination.

Their presence in this dead and tomblike place made no sense. Why would Hugh be here? They had exchanged harsh words at the end of their last meeting. The human had sent him away and told him never to return. Also, how could Iridaceae possibly have reached the Sublunary without his help? He had sent her back to the Night Lands before his capture... had he not?

The inscribed bullets lodged in his heart and shoulder flared with scorching agony as he shifted position, unused muscles creaking to life after so long frozen in place. The small part of his mind that maintained a measure of objectivity burned with humiliation at the echo of his desperate pleading for Hugh to *cut the bullets out* ringing in his ears.

A god did not *beg*.

Yet Morpheus would have said *anything*, done *anything* to rid himself of the torment. It had been slowly driving him mad as the hours spent in this oubliette slipped into days, into weeks, into *years*. How long had it been?

The knife Hugh had pulled out of his pocket clinked to the floor. Morpheus could have wailed with frustration despite the human's promises and pleas for patience. Then a new light pierced the darkness, and Iridaceae launched herself into flight, startled by the sudden glare. Hugh's hand fell away from Morpheus' chest as the human whirled to face the source.

Morpheus had been cold for what felt like an eternity, but the removal of that single point of warmth and living contact still sent a convulsive shiver through him.

"D-don't move," said the newcomer. "Or I'll shoot."

The voice was young. Female. Terrified.

Hugh rose to his feet slowly, his own handheld electric light playing over a red-haired human holding a firearm pointed at him.

A visceral memory of his capture sent a new wave of ice through Morpheus' veins—the explosions of noise as weapons fired... the impact of bullets against flesh. *Iridaceae*. Where was Iridaceae? He had to protect her—

"Deirdre," Hugh said, holding his hands outstretched to show he was unarmed. "What are you doing? Come on, now—there's no need for this. Talk to me. Why did you come back here? Tell me what you want."

"Why do you *think* I came back?" Anger and fear laced a tremor through the young woman's voice. "I couldn't get in here on my own! But you said you could. I've been camped at the edge of the woods waiting for you to show up for the last two nights!"

"That still doesn't tell me what you want," Hugh said, his tone determinedly level. "Why don't you put the gun down so we can talk?"

He took a careful step forward.

"Stay where you are!" the woman snapped. "Are you stupid? I want that... *thing*! I want its power! What kind of creature can live for eighty years without food or water or fresh air? Philomena said—"

She cut herself off with an audible click of teeth as her jaw clamped shut.

"Philomena said *what*?" Hugh's tone had gone from soothing to dangerous in an instant.

"It doesn't matter. That creature's power should have been my grandfather's. Instead, it'll be mine. Why the hell were you unchaining it? You'll get us all killed! Now step aside."

Hugh straightened, squaring his shoulders. His arms were still held out to the sides, but he stood firmly between Morpheus and the human holding the gun. "Sorry, but that won't be happening, luv. Turn around, walk out of here, and forget this place ever existed. There's nothing for you here but trouble."

The unexpected crack of sound pierced Morpheus' ears with a physical stab of pain, echoing against the fallen slabs of concrete. At the same instant, Hugh de Ferrers crumpled to the ground just beyond Morpheus' reach, flopping and jerking like a landed fish. A feral snarl peeled back Morpheus' lips. He reached for the woman's mind, intent on subduing her—but of course, nothing happened. The pain of the inscribed bullets binding his powers flared higher in response to the useless attempt, drawing a gasp of agony from his lips.

With an outraged hoot, Iridaceae swooped down from above, talons outstretched as she flew at the woman's face. The weapon clattered to the floor as its owner cried out in alarm, flailing wildly. The beam from the handheld light spun crazily as it fell from her grip as well. With a meaty thump of connecting flesh, Iridaceae's tiny body went flying sideways, impacting a collapsed section of rubble before falling to the ground, where she fluttered weakly and went still.

Incandescent rage rose in Morpheus' chest, hotter than the brand of the bullet in his heart. Breathing heavily, the woman whirled on him, her face bleeding from several deep scratches. The two fallen lights illuminated the scene between them.

The woman raised a shaking finger to point at him. "*You*. Whatever you are… you belong to *me*."

Morpheus glared up at her with more hatred than he'd ever felt for a mortal creature during the course of his long existence. Without breaking her gaze, he reached for the knife that had fallen from Hugh's grip and scooped it up with his freed hand. Turning the point inward, he plunged it into the wound in his chest, pressing it hilt-deep, twisting until the tip caught on metal. With a low growl, he tore the bullet free of his heart, slicing and digging until he could pry the tiny, rune-inscribed lump out of his flesh.

Blood welled, dripping down the gray covering of dust coating his skin. The woman gaped at him as though she couldn't conceive of such a thing being possible. The second bullet remained lodged in his shoulder, but the removal of the binding runes from his heart was enough to lift the edge of the heavy veil that had been thrown over his mind, separating his consciousness from the Night Lands.

He let the eternal Night boil up, funneling it through his damaged body until its impenetrable shadows poured from his eyes, flowing into the abandoned bunker like a rising black tide. The woman screamed as living darkness flooded around them, snuffing out the light shining from the two handheld electric torches and plunging the entire scene into the void.

As the shadows reached her, a connection flared to life between them, giving Morpheus the access into her mind he desired. Horror and second thoughts swirled together in her consciousness — far too late to save her. Morpheus swept the emotions aside, drowning her awareness in a sea of insanity, conjuring the darkest terrors from the realm of the oneiri to torment her.

Sobbing, she dropped to her knees and began patting the floor around her, feeling blindly through the flowing shadows until her hand hit the barrel of the discarded firearm. Darkness was no impediment to the God of Nightmares, so Morpheus watched impassively as she lifted the weapon, turned it to point toward her head, and pulled the trigger.

The explosion of noise this time was muffled by the swaddling darkness, as was the wet splatter of blood and bits of bone against the fallen rubble behind her. Her body hit the floor with a dull thud.

Teeth clenched, Morpheus allowed the shadows to slip back inside himself, pulling his remaining strength with them. The strain of calling forth even a fraction of his power with the second bullet still inside him had leached away every ounce of his vitality. Unable to hold himself up, he collapsed to the gritty floor. Hugh's body lay a few feet away, unmoving. He couldn't see Iridaceae at all from this vantage point, and his failing powers did not allow him to reach her with his mind.

Fresh blood from his chest wound seeped onto the cold concrete. Still bound by Thanatus' chains, his rage unassuaged, Morpheus closed his eyes and did the only thing he'd been able to do for the tortured eternity since he'd first been captured.

He waited.

TWENTY-NINE

2021 A.D.

HUGH GROANED, ROLLED onto his side, and proceeded to cough up what felt like at least half a gallon of frothy blood.

Next to fatal head wounds, punctured lungs were the absolute *worst*.

For a disorientating moment, he had no fucking idea where he was or what had happened. He was lying on a hard surface cushioned only by a layer of gritty dust. The shapes around him loomed, leaning at odd angles that made no sense. The only illumination came from two cone-shaped beams of light—one worryingly dim, and the other one flickering in and out at random intervals.

When he recognized the source as a pair of electric torches, more memories slotted into place with a resounding mental *click*. He scrambled into a sitting position, craning around until he found the prone form of Morpheus a few feet behind him, lying facedown at the very edge of the flickering torch beam.

The failing light illuminated one startling blue eye with an irregular, strobing pulse. That eye, staring straight at him, never blinked—nor did Morpheus move.

"Deirdre," Hugh croaked, the last few puzzle pieces falling into position. He whirled, following the flickering torch beam back to its source, to where a figure lay crumpled with the peculiar dishevelment of arms and legs unique to death. He fumbled for the other torch and lifted it. Its weak beam illuminated a distinctive pattern of blood splatter on the concrete, at what would have been head height behind the fallen figure.

With the practicality born of having lived through several centuries, including more wars than he cared to count, Hugh put Deirdre out of his mind as no longer a priority.

Morpheus' collapse was cause for considerable worry, but that blue eye was gazing at him with intent, rather than the fixed stare of death. His friend was alive, and that meant there was another immediate concern that took precedence.

"Iridaceae. Where's Iridaceae?" Hugh played the failing torch's light over the immediate area and swept it up toward the bunker's half-collapsed ceiling, searching for movement or the reflection of golden eyes in the dark. She'd flown away when Deirdre arrived—

Morpheus' eye flicked to a point of focus slightly to Hugh's left and past him, into the darkness beyond the edges of the torch beams. Heart in throat, Hugh turned to follow that unblinking gaze with his light.

"Oh, no." The little pile of feathers lay unmoving except for the rapid rise and fall of labored breathing.

Hugh rushed over, stumbling on legs that could have used a few more minutes to recover—nearly tripping over the ever-present debris littering the floor. Iridaceae lay in a heap, one wing twisted unnaturally out to the side of her body. Her eyes were huge, the pupils dilated until they almost swallowed the yellow gold of her irises despite the torch light shining in her face.

"Oh, *sweetheart*," Hugh murmured, shrugging out of his much-abused hoodie. He winced as the drying blood made it stick to the henley he was wearing underneath. The hoodie was bloodstained on both the front and back, he realized. Entrance and exit wounds. Deirdre's shot had gone straight through his body rather than bouncing off a rib, at least.

Leaning down, he carefully wrapped Iridaceae's small form in the thick fabric, trying not to jostle her broken wing. She let out a distressed cry as he lifted her carefully, but she settled as he carried her back to where Morpheus still lay partially chained.

After setting her down where Morpheus could see her and she could see him, Hugh fumbled in his pocket, relieved to find that the key was still where he'd shoved it earlier. It was the work of a couple of minutes to force open the remaining two dust-choked locks. He tossed the collar and the second wrist shackle aside in disgust.

For lack of any better ideas, he rolled and lifted Morpheus' upper body into his lap—only to freeze when the maneuver revealed a gaping wound to the left of Morpheus' sternum, where before there had been a neat bullet hole.

In Hugh's defense, he'd been dead a few minutes ago and shouldn't be expected to be at the top of his game quite yet… but it was only then that he noticed his knife clutched loosely in Morpheus' right hand, it's blade now coated in gore.

"What..." he asked blankly. "What did you..."

"The other bullet." It was more the shape of words than anything else. A puff of air past gray lips. "Get it... get it out..."

Had Morpheus dug the first bullet out of his own chest with Hugh's knife? Was that even possible?

Hugh gaped at him stupidly.

"Get it out... *please*..."

With a blink, Hugh kicked his brain back into gear, trying to force the fractured facts arrayed in front of him to make sense.

Fact: Morpheus had performed messy surgery on himself to remove a bullet that had been lodged in his heart for eighty-odd years. And it hadn't killed him. Because he was a god.

Fact: He'd been pleading for Hugh to remove the bullets—plural—from practically the first moment they'd found him.

Fact: Deirdre had gone from acting like a power-mad cartoon villain to—apparently—shooting herself in the head.

Fact: There was a second dark stain pointing to a small wound high in Morpheus' shoulder. Hugh couldn't see any other obvious marks on him, though the ever-present dust might be hiding a multitude of sins.

Reconciling it all was beyond him, but one thing was clear. If hacking a gaping chunk out of his own ribcage hadn't killed Morpheus, then Hugh prying a bullet out of his shoulder with considerably more care was unlikely to finish the job.

"All right," he said, hoping he hadn't gone completely round the bend. "All right. It's in your shoulder? That's the last one? I'll get it out, *leof*. I'll get it out of you right now."

The Old English endearment slipped out without his notice, a relic of his earliest years. He eased Morpheus to lie on his good side and steeled himself to palpate the area around the shoulder wound, feeling for the location of the bullet.

Morpheus didn't so much as flinch, and Hugh was unsure if he should be worried or impressed by the stoicism. The bullet had entered through the front of his friend's body at a slight angle, tearing through the flesh immediately beneath the clavicle and lodging against the heavy ball joint of the shoulder itself.

"Okay," he said, more for his own benefit than Morpheus'. "It's not that deep. I can do this."

The less said about the next ten minutes, the better.

The knife was filthy. Morpheus was filthy. Their surroundings were filthy. For a human, attempting field surgery under these conditions would have been tantamount to a death sentence.

But when the bullet popped free with an unpleasant sucking noise, Morpheus only groaned in relief, the tension melting out of his body. Rather than being weakened, he rolled into a sitting position and immediately turned to the owl bundled in Hugh's bloodstained hoodie.

"Iridaceae?" he asked hoarsely, reaching out a hand that hovered just shy of touching the rumpled feathers.

"Broken wing," Hugh said. "Not sure about any other injuries. I can find something in the first aid kit to use as a temporary splint, but then we'll have to move her. We need to get the hell out of this place."

He didn't like to think of what would happen when someone eventually noticed the destruction and discovered a dead body inside. With luck, they'd chalk it up to a really weird choice of location for a suicide. But whatever the case, Hugh wanted to be far away before that happened, and he needed to get these two somewhere safe.

He rummaged in his pack for fresh batteries for the torch. Once he had better light, he gingerly examined Iridaceae's wing, shushing her weak squawk of protest soothingly as he fashioned a splint for it and wrapped bandages around it.

"She's been stuck in owl form since she showed up a couple of months ago," he told Morpheus as he tucked Iridaceae back in the folds of his hoodie.

The God of Nightmares huddled on the floor nearby, a blanket wrapped around his gaunt body.

"The owl is her natural form," he said. "She requires my power to shift into her human guise."

Hugh nodded, because it wasn't any crazier than anything else that had happened in the last twenty-four hours. "Okay. Here's the thing. I'm worried about the effects of shock on a body that's so small. I think it might be better if she were in human form for her recovery—but not until we're out of here. It's going to be hard enough getting the three of us up that damaged staircase as it is."

Morpheus didn't move from his miserable hunched position. "I understand. Take her first. You have… transportation of some kind?"

Hugh did the mental math and made a snap decision. "I do, but it's a bit of a trek from the entrance to this place. I'm not comfortable leaving either of you alone that long. I'll take Iridaceae up to the entrance and set her just outside. Then I'll help you out and we'll go to the lorry together."

If he absolutely had to, Hugh was pretty sure he could fashion a sling out of the hoodie to support Iridaceae against his chest while he carried Morpheus on his back. Whether such a haughty creature would stoop to that level of humility was a hill he'd climb when and if he came to it.

"Come on, you daft feathered thing," he said, lifting Iridaceae into his arms with care. She made a weak chittering sound and didn't protest. "You know," he observed, "a lot of things make more sense if you're an owl who just happens to be able to turn into a human, rather than a human who just happens to be able to turn into an owl."

The path to the destroyed entrance was slightly less daunting going up than it had been coming down, at least. He stowed Iridaceae, wrapped in her makeshift swaddling, between two disturbed boulders at the edge of the gap he'd made with the backhoe.

"Screech if anything bigger than a mouse comes your way," he said, praying that none of the area wildlife would be willing to brave the newly disturbed site in the next few minutes. "I'll be *right* back."

Hurrying as fast as he dared without risking a fall and a broken ankle, Hugh half-climbed, half-slid down the pile of dirt and rubble to the remains of the concrete staircase. He'd tightened the loose bulb on Deirdre's torch and left it with Morpheus, unwilling to plunge his friend back into the same darkness where he'd been trapped for so long.

Even so, when he jogged back to the clear area where Morpheus had been chained, it was to find him staring fixedly at nothing, his eyes far away.

"Hey," Hugh said softly, not wanting to startle him. There was no response. Hugh crouched down in front of him, frowning. "*Morpheus.* You with me?"

The unearthly blue gaze snapped into focus, but it was haunted in a way Hugh recognized. He'd seen that look in the mirror on a fair few occasions over the centuries.

"I'm here. This is real," Hugh said, guessing at the cause. "We're leaving now, even if I have to carry your skinny arse out of here."

Weak offense chased away the haunted look, and Hugh cheered internally.

"I can walk," Morpheus said with great dignity. He rose to his feet and proceeded to stagger and nearly fall over as his knees failed to hold.

Hugh, who'd been prepared for something along those lines, caught him and dragged Morpheus' good arm across his shoulders for support. "Yeah, I can see that," he said, setting his feet to take most of Morpheus' insubstantial weight. "Come on, I don't want to leave Iridaceae alone up there for long."

In the end, it might have been faster if Hugh *had* carried him—but they made it to the surface and found Iridaceae unharmed, right where he'd left her. Morpheus seemed to gain a bit of steadiness as time went on, the three of them making their slow way along the grassy track toward the lorry.

Behind them, a cooling corpse lay inside an eighty-year-old tomb. Ahead lay *whatever came next.* With an injured owl cradled against his chest and a weakened, traumatized godling plastered against his left side, Hugh had absolutely no idea what that might entail.

THIRTY

2021 A.D.

MORPHEUS SAT IN a fugue state in the passenger seat of Hugh de Ferrers' motorized vehicle, the cloth-wrapped form of his injured familiar cradled in his arms. If only he could return Iridaceae to the Night Lands, he could heal her there. If only he could access his power without the attempt opening a pit inside him, sapping all his pathetic reserves of strength until his muscles trembled and his sight tunneled in, gray at the edges.

If only… *if only.*

Hugh's low muttering penetrated Morpheus' musings. The human was hunched over the machine's controls like a defensive vulture. "Just so the rozzers don't try to pull me over for a busted tail lamp or something. God, that's *all* we need."

Iridaceae gave a mournful hoot as the vehicle jolted over a rough spot in the road, shuddering in Morpheus' arms. Every one of his senses was heightened. The abrupt transition from decades of *nothing,* to the sudden reintroduction of *everything,* jarred at his nerves. The rumble of the internal combustion engine felt deafening. The smell of unburned hydrocarbons was choking. The lights illuminating a wedge of the road ahead were dazzling. The brush of the woolen blanket loosely encircling his shoulders might as well have been sandpaper against his filthy skin.

He wished to be *clean.*

Oh, how he wished to be clean.

Iridaceae tried to ruffle her feathers, only to shudder again as the attempt jarred her shattered wing. Morpheus swallowed an upswelling of rage aimed at the dead woman buried in the prison behind them, aware that the impulse was useless. He stroked fingertips over the soft feathers of Iridaceae's head. The owl blinked up at him, her pupils blown wide.

"Easy, luv," Hugh said, his eyes never wavering from the road. "Only ten more minutes and we're home, I promise."

Morpheus squinted and turned his face away as twin beams of blinding light approached, moving in the opposite direction to Hugh's vehicle. The beams passed by so close that it seemed they might collide. Hugh didn't react, implying that such interactions on the road were normal.

They had encountered only a handful of other vehicles, thankfully. Another few minutes, and Hugh turned the unwieldy mechanical conveyance onto a narrower track; one that eventually led to a small cottage hidden among old-growth trees.

"This is my place," said the human. "A poor thing, but mine own." He turned a small key set in the mysterious array of dials and switches before him, after which the all-pervasive rumble of the engine died away. "I'm going to leave the lights on so I can see what I'm doing while I get you both inside."

Morpheus would have preferred darkness, but he said nothing. Hugh shot him a worried, sidelong glance before opening his door with an ear-splitting shriek of metal hinges. He hopped down and jogged around the front, the twin lights illuminating the dark stain of dried blood on his clothing.

When he opened Morpheus' door with a similar unpleasant squeal, Morpheus handed Iridaceae down to him without a word. Hugh took her, shooting Morpheus another fleeting, worried look.

"I'll be right back. Don't try to move."

Morpheus waited until the pair disappeared into the modest structure before grasping the doorframe and slithering out of the seat. His strength deserted him the moment his bare feet touched the ground, the blanket sliding from his shoulders as he clutched at the metal frame of the vehicle to stay upright.

He was still locked in that ignominious position when Hugh returned. The human's lips thinned, but he made no comment—only stooping to retrieve the fallen blanket and replacing it around Morpheus' shoulders before wrapping an arm around him and leading him through the beams of painful light to the door of the cottage.

The inside was homey and unprepossessing. A rather cramped sitting room boasted a battered green sofa, along with some bookshelves and a heavy wooden desk with a matching chair. Hugh led him to the sofa, where Iridaceae already lay nestled on a sagging cushion in her makeshift swaddling.

A black cat with a tattered ear sat stiff with tension on the desk nearby, its tail lashing. Hugh followed Morpheus' gaze to the creature.

"It's all right," he said. "Baphometh and Iridaceae have what you could call an understanding. *Shoo*, Baph. Cat hair won't help this situation."

The cat let out an offended meow and leapt down from the desk, scampering out the door.

After depositing Morpheus next to his injured familiar, Hugh straightened. "Sorry… sorry. I'll just be another minute. No neighbors nearby—but even so, I don't want to risk attracting attention with those lights on the lorry."

He rushed out, leaving Morpheus and his familiar in welcome silence, broken only by a low, electronic hum coming from some piece of incomprehensible human technology lying on the desk like a dull silver tablet.

As promised, Hugh returned within moments, turning on several lamps around the perimeter of the room as he entered. Morpheus winced, hating himself for the show of weakness—but of course, human eyes would need better light for assessing and treating an injury.

Hugh crouched in front of Morpheus, looking up at him earnestly. The regard of those warm brown eyes stirred… *something*… inside him, where nothing but cold and emptiness had dwelt for so long. He chased the sensation, but it evaporated into blankness within moments.

The human's brows drew together in concern. "Is there anything wrong with you that will cause catastrophic harm if it's left unaddressed for a little while longer?"

"No," Morpheus rasped, painfully aware that only time and rest could mend what had been broken in him.

Hugh gave a slow nod. "Good. Next question. Iridaceae requires your power to shift into her human form, right? I need to remove the splint from her wing first. But, once I do, are you strong enough to help her?"

A muscle in Morpheus' jaw jumped. He could not help her as he wished to, by taking her to the gods' realm where she might be properly healed. But pushing the shift of form would not require as much power.

"I will help her change," he managed, still in that strange, hoarse voice that sounded nothing like his.

Another nod, and Hugh turned his attention to Iridaceae, making soothing noises as he unwrapped the bandages holding the splints around her wing in place. When he was done, he let out a deep breath and stood. "Ready. Brace yourself, sweetheart. I'm so sorry about this."

Morpheus lowered himself to kneel in front of the couch and peeled back the blood-stiffened cloth Iridaceae was wrapped in. As before, reaching for his power drained every bit of strength from his body. He let it slip away without attempting to hold onto it, his vision fading to blackness as his hearing grew distorted and distant.

The faintest hint of his connection to his familiar teased his awareness, and he grasped it with both hands, channeling the trickle of power to her. For a moment, he didn't know if it had been enough. Then an all-too-human arm circled his neck. Muffled female sobs pierced the cotton wool stuffed in his ears as Iridaceae tucked her head under his chin and wept.

"Easy—lie back now, Iridaceae." Hugh's worried voice entered the strange echo chamber of Morpheus' senses. "He's safe. You're both safe now, I promise. But I need to splint your arm again. And I'm so sorry, but it's going to hurt."

Morpheus gathered the last of his strength and brushed invisible fingers across Iridaceae's mind, sending her into a deep sleep.

"*Shit*," Hugh cursed, then paused. "Oh. Was that you?"

Morpheus managed a nod.

"Okay. That's… um, that's good. Just rest for a bit while I work. I'll get her arm sorted and move her to the guest room. It's not much, but the bed's comfortable."

Hands on his shoulders eased Morpheus to the side, out of the way. He could summon no indignation at the manhandling, too focused on the twin impressions of warm skin against skin through the cold and the filth cloaking him.

Time drifted, formless and vague. He was surprised when the hands returned, settling him with his back against the wood frame and soft upholstery of the couch.

"I tucked her in and she's down for the count, I think," Hugh said—and at least Morpheus' hearing had returned to something like normalcy. "From the looks of it, you should rest, too."

Morpheus hadn't even noticed Hugh carrying Iridaceae from the room, so disconnected was he from his surroundings. Still, he shook his head in negation. "Clean," he mumbled, fighting to keep his words from slurring. "I must be... *clean*."

There was a pause.

"Yeah," Hugh said. "Okay. You're a right mess, and no mistake. Guess I can understand the request."

The blanket had fallen away again, but this time Hugh didn't bother to retrieve it. He rose, tugging Morpheus up with him, and dragged one of Morpheus' arms over his shoulders as he'd done at the bunker.

"Come on. I installed a shower in the boot room... got tired of coming home covered in mud and dragging it into the house with me. We'll rinse off the worst of the dust, and then you can have a proper bath if you want."

The ache of pathetic desire he felt at the prospect was but one fresh humiliation among many. Nevertheless, Morpheus meekly allowed himself to be led through the modest cottage, one slow step at a time. The lure of hot water—such a very human luxury—was a siren call that kept him lifting one foot after the other, leaning on Hugh's sturdy strength as they swayed and stumbled their way toward the promise of clean skin and blessed, blessed rest.

THIRTY-ONE

2021 A.D.

HUGH HAD NEVER been so thankful for his self-indulgence in the form of an on-demand tankless water heater in the cottage bathroom. It was the medieval peasant in him, he supposed—but even centuries later, he was still obsessed by the ready availability of things like hot water and central heating.

At least thinking about modern plumbing helped him in his quest *not* to think about the naked Greek god draped against him. *Impersonal*, he coached himself for approximately the hundredth time in the last twenty minutes. *Keep it impersonal.*

And truly, even after sluicing off a half-inch thick coating of dust and filth in Hugh's shower in the boot room, the God of Nightmares was a rather pathetic and bedraggled figure.

Hugh could infer that Morpheus didn't need food or water to survive, given that he'd had neither for some eighty years. But whether it was starvation, or some other lack beyond Hugh's mortal ken, his body had become gaunt to the point of being skeletal. He had no beard, and his messy nest of dark hair hadn't grown, but it had become lank and dull, falling over his eyes.

Morpheus could barely stand under his own power. Hugh had, by necessity, shucked his boots and rolled up the sleeves of his Henley so he could reach through the half-closed shower curtain and help Morpheus stay upright. The warm water sluiced over his hunched form, disappearing in a gray-brown stream down the drain. Hugh was fairly certain that concrete dust didn't resolidify after it got wet, but his septic system still might never be the same.

Practical upshot—helping his weak and debilitated guest get clean and comfortable should in no way have had Hugh's stomach dipping and fluttering in a series of complicated roller coaster twists.

And yet... *Greek god.*

Mysterious stranger.

Naked, wet mysterious stranger.

Hugh gritted his teeth, maintaining the bare minimum of contact necessary to keep Morpheus from face-planting as they traversed his back hallway toward the bathroom.

The room wasn't much, really. However, the clawfoot tub was an antique, and with the tankless water heater, it would stay warm until even a god ended up with pruny fingers.

"Sorry," Hugh muttered, easing his immortal burden through the doorway in an awkward sideways dance. He led Morpheus to the toilet and sat him down on the closed lid for lack of any better options. "Wait here for a second while I get the water going. I want to look at your wounds."

"They are of no import," Morpheus said, in that same, rasping half-whisper that seemed to be all he could muster since his rescue.

"Glad to hear it," Hugh said. "In that case, checking them will only take a minute."

Morpheus blinked crystalline eyes at him and did not reply.

Hugh bustled around, relieved that the bathroom was at least clean, if a bit cluttered. He started the water running, holding his wrist under it. When the temperature was a few degrees above blood-warm, he pulled his hand away and plugged the drain so it could fill. After dragging out a clean washcloth and draping a couple of fresh towels over the warming rack—another amazing invention he hadn't been able to resist—he returned to crouch in front of the thin figure slouched on the bog.

Steeling himself, he touched Morpheus' shoulder, urging him to straighten and turn toward the lights over the vanity. "Here. Let me see."

Morpheus meekly let himself be positioned—yet another little jolt of wrongness in this horrifically wrong situation. The stranger Hugh had known for eight hundred years had never struck him as *pliant*.

He was pliant enough in some of your dreams, whispered a deeply unhelpful little voice inside Hugh's head.

He clenched his teeth harder and focused on the gaunt chest in front of him, every rib standing out in stark relief. Pale marble skin, tender and new as a babe's, covered an ugly dip that marred the otherwise perfect lines of Morpheus' ribcage. It couldn't even be called a scar. Hugh suspected that it would be completely healed within hours, as though it had never existed.

Indeed, he couldn't even find the shoulder wound, and he had to stop and think very hard for a moment to be sure he was looking on the correct side. He was less shocked than most people would have been. Heaven only knew that he'd seen his own wounds heal with supernatural speed over the centuries. Still, it was jarring.

"Anything else I need to know about?" he asked, rather than make a fuss about it. "Other injuries? Magic stuff?"

Perfect dark brows furrowed. "Magic... *stuff?*" Morpheus echoed in a weak tone of offense.

Hugh shrugged. "Well, I don't know what else to call it, now do I? It sounds like the bullets wouldn't have been such an issue if not for the supernatural gubbins, right?"

Morpheus consciously smoothed his expression to one of blankness. "The bullets were engraved with sigils and binding runes. They have been removed, along with the chains. Therefore, there is no more *magic stuff* affecting me." The words dripped with contempt; the effect somewhat lessened by the fact that their speaker resembled nothing so much as a half-drowned cat.

"Okay," Hugh said. "So, you just need... what? Rest?"

Morpheus' shoulders slumped. He looked away and gave a small, reluctant nod.

"Don't knock it," Hugh told him. "We'd be in a lot worse position if you needed some long-lost artifact from an ancient temple in order to recover."

Morpheus dipped his chin, still not looking at him. To Hugh's surprise, one corner of his lips turned up, a faint huff of breath escaping that might, in another world, have been an expression of amusement.

"And yet," said the god, "if I told you I required a golden chalice from the summit of Mount

Olympus, you would drop everything and attempt to retrieve it. Despite the inauspicious ending to our last meeting."

Hugh sat back on his heels, startled. "Well... I mean... I'd probably need some additional information and a bit of time to try and organize an expedition." He swallowed, not prepared to delve into their last meeting with such little notice. "Last time, I... uh... might have behaved like a bit of a twat. Not that you weren't exhibiting some twattish tendencies as well, mind you."

"And still, you harbored Iridaceae and risked yourself to find me," Morpheus said softly, looking at him as though he was some kind of complicated puzzle.

"Course I did," Hugh said. "Just because you have a row with your friend, it doesn't mean you leave him in the lurch next time he needs you." Now it was his turn to look away. "I'm just sorry it took me eighty years."

Morpheus' confused frown returned. "You were not to know."

Hugh scrubbed a hand over his eyes and stood up. "Should've known, though. I had a nightmare in 1940. First one I'd had in ages," he said gruffly. "Thought you finally got sick of coddling me. I should've realized it meant you were in trouble somehow."

Morpheus bowed his head again, his eyelids slipping closed. Hugh tried not to stare at the dark sweep of lashes against alabaster skin. Tried, and failed.

"You were not to know," he said again, a bare whisper.

Something thick gathered in Hugh's throat, and he had to cough a couple of times before he could speak. "It's in the past now. All of it. Come on. The bath's about ready, I think."

Morpheus allowed himself to be helped across to the generous tub and lowered into it. He sank down with an audible sigh, clouds of steam rising around him.

"Nothing quite like a hot bath when you've had a shit time of things," Hugh said lamely, straightening.

Morpheus made a low, humming noise that might have been agreement, sliding down and letting his head fall back to rest against the edge of the tub, his eyes closed. Hugh absolutely did not stare at the pale column of throat the movement exposed, the prominent Adam's apple jutting a few inches above the waterline.

More words jumbled in Hugh's throat, jostling for freedom.

Don't say it. Don't say it. Don't say it.

"I could help you wash your hair if you want," he blurted.

There was a beat of silence, during which Hugh rapidly cycled through possible methods of temporary suicide—ones that might leave him unable to hear or understand the inevitable cold dismissal that would surely be coming his way any moment now.

"That would be… agreeable," Morpheus said, an instant before Hugh would have gone searching for the nearest handy shotgun. He hadn't even opened his eyes, still soaking in the warmth of the bath.

"Oh," Hugh said brilliantly. "Um."

One eye cracked open to look at him.

"It's just, maybe I should go check on Iridaceae?" Hugh went on rapidly, aware that he was blushing like a maiden.

"Iridaceae will not wake until I allow it," Morpheus said, lifting his head to look at Hugh properly. "And I will know if anything is amiss with her in the meantime."

"Oh," he said again.

And that was how Hugh de Ferrers—thirteenth century peasant and occasional vandal of secret military property—found himself sitting on a chair borrowed from the kitchen with a pitcher of warm water and a bottle of eucalyptus scented shampoo, washing the silky-soft hair of a creature who'd probably come into existence at the same time the universe had.

"Tilt your head back," he said, ignoring the soft, hysterical gibbering in the ancient reptile part of his brain.

Morpheus hummed again and complied, the graceful line of his neck once more calling to something in Hugh that was both dark, and better left unexamined.

Hugh silently recited cricket statistics, on the theory that they were even less interesting than football statistics would have been. When he was certain no suds remained among the night-black strands of hair, he set the pitcher aside and grabbed a warm towel.

"You know," he said, aware that he was babbling, "I lived in the Blue Mountains in Pennsylvania for a while after I left New York. Coal mining area, mostly—but it was honest work. They had this legend there."

"*Ewige Jaeger*," Morpheus murmured. "The Eternal Hunter. I know of it." Hugh stared at him, and Morpheus raised an eyebrow. "It is an old tale. One common in much of Northern Europe. Doubtless it arrived in the New World with Germanic immigrants."

Hugh blinked. "About a bloke who loved hunting so much that he was cursed to pursue a ghostly stag for the rest of eternity without ever catching it."

Morpheus tilted his head. "Usually, it is told with a fox in that part of the world, not a stag."

Hugh nodded. "Yes, some places called it a fox, but in the town where I lived, it was a white stag." He chewed the inside of his lip, remembering the way he'd felt the first time he'd heard an old man tell the tale around a campfire. "I sympathized with the hunter rather a lot," he finished.

Morpheus' expression grew hooded. "Did you indeed?"

Hugh forged ahead, because there was a god in his bathtub and an owl with a broken arm in his spare bedroom, and tomorrow he would have to hide the evidence that he was in any way involved with a dead body in an abandoned WWII bunker.

Also, there was Philomena. And right now, he couldn't bear to deal with any of it.

"Yeah. I did. Always daydreaming after the stag I could never catch."

Morpheus rose from the bath with strength he hadn't possessed half an hour ago, taking the towel from Hugh's grasp.

"And now the stag eats from your hand," Morpheus said, in a tone Hugh couldn't parse.

His stomach flipped, and he swallowed hard to settle it.

"I, um, didn't offer you any food," he said, scrabbling for something—*anything*—that wasn't this particular conversation. Even though he'd been the one to start it, idiot that he was. "Do you need to eat or drink?"

"No," Morpheus said.

"Do you *want* to eat or drink?" Hugh tried.

"Not at the moment, thank you."

"Then you should probably rest now," he said, because it seemed like the safest option. "Are you feeling better? You seem a bit steadier than before."

"It appears your attentions are restorative," Morpheus said, and Hugh utterly refused to think too closely about the words, because there was dangerous and then there was *dangerous*.

"Hey, like I said, nothing quite like a hot bath when you've gone through a rough patch." He kept his tone light and hovered a hand near Morpheus' elbow as he stepped out of the tub, unneeded though it apparently was now.

The ugly divot in Morpheus' ribcage was completely gone.

Morpheus ran the towel over himself in a perfunctory fashion, as though unconcerned by his own dampness. When he was done, he let it fall, looking mildly perplexed when it puddled wetly on the floor. Maybe he'd expected it to magically fly over to the towel rack and fold itself, Hugh thought.

"Leave it," he said. "Sorry—I didn't think earlier. I can try to find a robe or something for you…"

Morpheus dragged his scowling attention away from the offending towel, his expression softening as his gaze landed on Hugh's face. "What matter? You've already seen me unclothed. Modesty is a human affectation."

He was upright under his own power, but exhaustion still lurked behind that unearthly gaze.

"Right, then," Hugh said, hoping that the tips of his ears weren't as red-hot as they felt. "Bedroom."

He led the way, listening for any unevenness of gait that might indicate Morpheus still needed his support—but his companion followed him silently. Opening the door to his bedroom and turning on the light, Hugh winced a bit at the mess.

"Here you go," he said, as Morpheus brushed past him into the room, looking around the very human space with vague interest. "Anyway, just… make yourself at home, okay? Let me know if you need anything, and, uh, I'll just leave you to it, I suppose—"

A long-fingered hand darted out, catching Hugh's wrist as he made to turn and leave.

Hugh jerked his head around in surprise, finding himself face to face with a pair of blue eyes set in sharp, finely sculpted features.

Once again, Morpheus was studying him like an unfamiliar puzzle box. "For one who is so forward in dreams," he said mildly, "you are surprisingly reticent in the waking world, Hugh de

Ferrers. After eight hundred years, you have caught your stag. Will you not now claim your prize?"

THIRTY-TWO

2021 A.D.

WORSHIP. MORPHEUS HAD not experienced it in such direct fashion in a very long time. For all that the humans needed him and his fellow gods to hold up the invisible framework that formed their lives—birth and death, fear and fantasy, and, yes, dreams—large parts of the world had forsaken them in favor of other religions… other gods.

As long as mortal creatures escaped to a different world in their sleep, Morpheus would continue to exist. Whether he was in his palace in the Night Lands or trapped alone in an underground prison with his powers bound by an inscribed bullet, he was still the God of Nightmares and Dreams.

He had not, however, fully appreciated the influence that those dreamers held over him, in turn.

In the absence of any living contact—physical, mental, or spiritual—he had grown weak beyond the bearing of it. Even now, his power hovered just outside of his reach, the fragile physical vessel in which he'd been trapped for so long unable to support more than a tiny trickle.

And the touch of a single human being, an immortal man who'd dreamed for centuries of bringing Morpheus down to Earth, was the first infusion of strength and warmth he'd felt since the humans had sealed the entrance of their bunker, leaving him trapped in the dark with the rotting corpses of soldiers buried under the rubble.

Morpheus hadn't expected Hugh de Ferrers to balk at the invitation being offered. How many times had the man crashed into the world of dreams, intent on debauching him with such single-minded focus that Morpheus often had to wrench himself free of the fantasy by main force?

Now, the human stared at Morpheus' grip on his wrist with eyes wide as dinner plates, a hot flush rising to his cheeks. Morpheus *needed* that heat. Already, the warmth of the bath was fading, the damp, inescapable chill of the bunker threatening to reassert itself.

Gods sometimes took human lovers. Perhaps Morpheus himself had never indulged before now, but Phantasos was notorious for the practice, and even dour Thanatus had done so on occasion.

It was not such an unheard-of thing as all that.

"Erm," Hugh said, his wide eyes darting up from Morpheus' fingers encircling his wrist to meet his gaze. "When you say, '*in dreams*,' does that mean…"

He trailed off, his flush creeping higher.

"I am the God of Dreams, Hugh de Ferrers," Morpheus said patiently. "While I am not personally present in every nighttime flight of fancy, for a human to dream of me directly is rather… *singular*. It does tend to draw my attention."

The ruddy spots of color on the human's cheeks drained away abruptly, leaving pale white in their wake. Hugh opened his mouth and closed it, then did it a second time.

Finally, he managed to form words. "Are you telling me that when I dreamed of you, I was actually... with... *you?*"

Abruptly, Morpheus grew concerned that their roles were about to be reversed, and he might be called on to support the suddenly pasty-faced man to his bed rather than the other way around.

"You puzzled out my identity long ago, did you not?" Morpheus asked. "Much to my chagrin, I might add."

Hugh continued to stare at him. "Well, yes, but..." His words trailed off again, but after a moment he blinked and shook his head briskly. "Look, you need rest and I need to go have a minor mental breakdown over this..." He hesitated, waving his free hand around. "*All* of this, whatever this is."

Morpheus did not release his wrist.

"... And you're still not letting me go," Hugh concluded.

"I am not," Morpheus agreed.

Some sort of complicated inner conflict flickered across the human's expression for only a moment before he said, "Oh, *fuck it,*" and spun Morpheus around, shoving him against the wall just to the right of the doorframe.

That blessed human warmth returned, pressing all along his front as Hugh covered Morpheus' body with his own, caging him in place and fastening heated lips on what would have been Morpheus' vulnerable pulse point, had he been mortal.

"Fuck... *fuck,*" Hugh murmured against the sensitive skin. "I thought I'd lost you. After last time... I knew I'd mucked things up the moment you disappeared. And then you were gone, and I thought that was it. I'd never see you again."

The words vibrated across the delicate nerves running beneath the skin of Morpheus' throat, awakening senses that had barricaded themselves away to survive the decades of terrible cold and quiet. He let his head fall back, exposing more skin to the sensation.

"I would have come," he said reluctantly, unsure why the admission rankled.

Hugh let out a sharp breath, the puff of air cool against the dampness left by his lips earlier. Morpheus shuddered, unbidden. Then, with a pained noise, the human pushed away. More cold air shivered along his front at the sudden loss of Hugh's body heat.

"This," Hugh said, pointing between them. "Is this… supposed to be some kind of reward? For services rendered? You saw what was in my dreams, so now you think you have to indulge me with this as a thank-you for getting you out of that bunker? Because if so, you can take your *services rendered* and shove them right up your—"

"No," Morpheus said, cutting him off.

Hugh's jaw snapped shut. Possibly because of the strange way that single negative word had emerged from Morpheus' throat—broken and hoarse.

"Then… why?" Hugh demanded. His tone was plaintive. "*Eight hundred years* and you've never so much as looked at me twice. You were like a bloody monk!"

Morpheus blinked. *I warned you about that stick up your arse*, whispered a voice that sounded disturbingly like Phantasos. *How's your precious dignity doing now?*

"I have looked at you twice," he admitted. "More than twice, in fact."

Hugh, standing a step away now, shook his head in apparent disbelief. "When?" he asked. "When I was fast asleep and didn't know you were anything other than a figment of my overactive imagination?"

When you lay injured and starving in a French prison, Morpheus thought. *When you confronted my brother despite your terror of him. When I watched over you in a Scottish mortuary.*

"I am not prone to displays of unbridled emotion," he said stiffly. "That is not my nature."

Hugh stared at him. "Really? Wow, I hadn't noticed." The human took a deep, centering breath and ran a hand through his unruly brown hair. "Look, I think it'd be best if I left you alone to rest now. This has been… a hell of a day, to put it mildly."

The cold pricked at Morpheus' bare skin.

"I have been *alone* for eighty years," he said.

Hugh froze for a moment, and then the human looked at him—really *looked*—rather than seeing only what he assumed was there.

"Oh," he whispered. "*Oh.*"

Beneath that startled regard, a faint echo of the previous warmth chased away some of Morpheus' chill.

"I told you earlier that your attentions are restorative," Morpheus said. "That was not an untruth."

For a long moment, Hugh appeared lost for words. Eventually, he spoke.

"You said you didn't need food or drink." The words emerged slowly, as though he was picking them with care, one at a time. "But you were stronger after… after I helped you bathe." He swallowed, his throat bobbing. "So, there's something else you need, like humans need food?"

"Worship," Morpheus said simply, aware that many humans would find such an implication offensive.

Hugh swallowed again, convulsively.

"God fucking help me," he rasped.

Morpheus raised a slow eyebrow in response to the blasphemous imprecation, and the flush from earlier colored Hugh's face once more.

"Get on the damned bed," said the human. "Are you sure Iridaceae will be all right?"

"She is sleeping peacefully," Morpheus assured him, "and will continue to do so."

He crossed the room and got on the damned bed. After a slight pause, Hugh followed, placing a hand in the center of Morpheus' chest where the bullet had torn through his flesh. Morpheus allowed himself to be born down to the mattress, closing his eyes as warmth spread outward from the contact.

The edge of the bed dipped under the weight of a second body.

"Smite me if you don't like something, I guess," Hugh said hoarsely.

"I will not smite you," Morpheus replied without opening his eyes.

"Doesn't matter anyway, does it?" Hugh muttered. "It's not as though it would stick."

The palm pressed to his chest slid downward, radiating heat and rough with calluses.

THIRTY-THREE

2021 A.D.

HUGH'S HEART POUNDED like the thundering hooves of a racehorse, the pulse of blood through his veins making him dizzy. It was probably a good thing that an aneurysm wouldn't stick any more than a good, old-fashioned deific smiting would. Not that the knowledge would make collapsing from some sort of catastrophic cardiopulmonary failure any less humiliating.

The tableau in the bedroom had the sort of surreal haziness of a time out of time. Hugh wasn't foolish enough to picture this as anything more than it was. All he could do was cram the future inside a box and hide it away someplace dark, out of sight. Perhaps this night was all he would have for the next hundred years… but for now, it was still *his*.

The marble perfection of skin beneath his hand was cool to the touch. Morpheus' body was completely hairless; still painfully gaunt after his decades-long imprisonment. Yet now that he really looked, Hugh could see that not only had his wounds healed, but his bony frame was already beginning to fill out.

Morpheus' physical proportions certainly befitted a Greek god. Even starved for so long of whatever esoteric sustenance he drew from mortals, his body was chiseled perfection of the sort that would have made Leonardo da Vinci weep. Every bone, every wiry muscle, every tendon and sinew begged Hugh to explore it in detail.

The catch and drag of his work-roughened hand, as he slid it over prominent ribs and down a painfully concave stomach, felt like a kind of blasphemy. Surely nothing should touch such pale, unblemished flesh except the finest of silks, the softest of furs. And yet, the figure on Hugh's bed arched like a cat, pushing into the contact. Morpheus' head fell back, baring his slender throat—his Adam's apple prominent in profile.

Unable to quell the impulse despite the thrill of superstitious fear the prospect sent through him, Hugh stretched out his free hand, sliding it upwards from a lean pectoral to dance over the sharp jut of a prominent collarbone. He settled his cupped palm over that vulnerable throat, resting it there as his other hand traveled the final few inches downward to encircle a perfect, pale cock.

Morpheus made a small, punched-out noise as Hugh gently pinned him in place—the sharp exhalation of air vibrating through his windpipe beneath Hugh's light grip. His cock was barely half-hard at first, but within the circle of Hugh's callused fingers, the cool marble flesh swelled, taking on a hint of borrowed warmth.

"You beautiful bastard," Hugh said hoarsely, as that perfect male member grew heavy and thick in his hand. "Bet you've got people lined up for a mile begging to do this. '*Worship*,' my arse. More like finally bringing you down to Earth."

He gave an experimental stroke, wringing a low hum of satisfaction from his victim. Morpheus was unexpectedly docile beneath his touch; eyes closed and focus visibly turned inward. Hugh held him down with the merest suggestion of restraint and worked him steadily toward his peak, relishing the tiny quivers and twitches that he seemed unable to stifle.

Then, because several centuries of immortality did have the unfortunate side effect of distorting one's sense of risk tolerance all to hell, he waited until the body on his bed tensed, its final crisis approaching… and released Morpheus' cock in favor of running his palm over every expanse of skin he could reach, stroking firmly.

This, presumably, would be when the smiting happened if it were going to. But Morpheus only lay there, muscles drawn taut, lips faintly parted as though he were drinking in the sensation of being balanced on the peak and left dangling there.

Something about the sight made Hugh realize just how hard he was inside his own trousers — painfully so, his erection throbbing and pulsing in time with his wildly elevated heartbeat. But doing anything about it would have meant breaking contact with at least one hand, and that prospect was far more painful than a case of constricted blue balls.

So, Hugh ignored his own urgency, teasing fingers upward to scrape a nail lightly over a pebbled pink nipple, then downward to knead and tug at Morpheus' velvety scrotum. He slipped a finger farther back until he encountered the soft pucker of his captive's entrance, describing ever-decreasing circles around the rim until his fingertip dipped inside.

A nearly inaudible moan vibrated beneath Hugh's palm, and he cursed himself for not having any oil or lube within arm's reach. Reluctantly, he abandoned that particular exploration. Tonight, he was unwilling to see Morpheus suffer any form of discomfort beyond the torment of a delayed orgasm.

Some of the terrible tension had leached from the god's muscles, so Hugh returned to his cock again, working his foreskin up and down, the glistening head of his prick peeking out with every deliberate stroke.

Time held no meaning as Hugh pushed Morpheus' body to the edge over and over again, marveling at the way strength and vitality returned to the lithe, rapturous form as he watched. It might have been hours—*must* have been hours, as the faintest hint of gray dawn filtered through the curtains on the bedroom's single window. Hugh's own lust was a dull, background ache of desire, mostly forgotten in favor of drinking in the perfection before him.

A single miscalculation—one twisting stroke too many—and the hazy fever dream reached its inevitable conclusion. Morpheus' spine arched into a perfect bow, his muscles shuddering as he pulsed and spent over Hugh's hand, his own belly, and even his perfect, hairless chest.

He was utterly silent as he came. The only sound breaking the peace of the bedroom was the strangled groan Hugh couldn't quite manage to stifle. His dick throbbed, demanding relief now that his focus was no longer on the delicate dance of his partner's stimulation and subsequent denial. He ignored the sensation with difficulty, still cupping Morpheus' softening cock with one hand while sliding the other up to brush the backs of his fingers over a cut-glass cheekbone.

The soft fan of Morpheus' dark eyelashes fluttered against his cheeks as Hugh hovered over him, watching his face intently. Every ounce of tension was gone from his limbs, and the body that had been gaunt mere hours ago was now merely slender—sleek muscles quiescent underneath glowing skin.

Hugh drank in the sight like a man dying of thirst, even as a slow sense of dread crept in around the edges of his consciousness. Morpheus' startling, crystal-blue eyes opened languidly, no hint of post-coital muzziness in that piercing gaze. He lifted one long-fingered hand to brush along Hugh's stubbled cheek, mirroring Hugh's earlier gesture.

"Your loyalty will not be forgotten, Hugh de Ferrers," Morpheus said, his voice no longer the weak rasp it had been before. "Nor will it go unrewarded."

In the next instant, the body on the bed dissolved into nothingness beneath Hugh's touch, that blue gaze the last thing to disappear. Hugh's breath caught as he stared at the empty mattress. His eyes flew to his left hand—now completely clean and free of drying stickiness. Vertigo assailed him for a moment; then he was upright, stumbling toward the guest room where he'd laid Iridaceae's sleeping body.

It, too, was vacant—the sheets rumpled around a small depression in the center of the twin bed. Hugh sat down abruptly in the room's solitary chair. He stared at the deserted space, his heart contracting

in a painful rhythm as he contemplated the blank,
empty expanse of the next hundred years.

THIRTY-FOUR

2021 A.D.

HUGH SAT NEXT to the empty bed in his small guest room for what was probably far too long a time. He stared with a blank gaze at the rumpled sheets where Iridaceae had lain, because the prospect of getting up and returning to the bed where Morpheus had lain felt far too painful.

His bedroom.

His bed.

Morpheus had been writhing naked on his bed.

And now he was gone. Hugh had a feeling he was going to be sleeping on the couch for the foreseeable future.

Not that he could afford the time for sleep right now, despite having been up for more than twenty-four hours straight already. His dick chose that moment to remind him — unhelpfully — that it, too, had been *up* for several hours earlier. He ignored it, because the prospect of jerking himself off over memories of Morpheus arching and trembling beneath his touch made him feel vaguely queasy.

Whatever last night had been, it wasn't fuel for his personal wank bank.

Baphometh padded in and leapt up on the rumpled bed, inserting himself into Hugh's line of sight. He gave a pitiful meow of the sort implying imminent starvation — as if the little beast didn't spend his nights hunting rodents in the forest and generally terrorizing the local wildlife.

Still, it was the impetus Hugh needed to finally tear himself away from the memory of the last few hours. He had to focus on practicalities. There was a destroyed security fence and an open bunker with a dead body in it—all less than fifty miles from his house. He still had a rented lorry and backhoe parked on his property, incriminating evidence to anyone who might think to look.

Dierdre was still dead. And Philomena was still—

Actually, Hugh wasn't one hundred percent sure yet *how* Philomena played into all of this. Not beyond the fact that she'd apparently sent Dierdre to stake out the bunker while armed with a gun.

No… right now, his priority had to be cleaning the mud off the backhoe he'd rented. Then he could return it in pristine condition to the equipment company in Ipswich, under the guise of his fictional alter-ego, Howard Farrington.

Baphometh meowed again.

Well, that and feeding the cat, apparently. "Come on, you horrible beast," he said, reluctantly rising to go and rejoin the real world.

—◆—

Even some four hundred years later, Ipswich brought back unpleasant memories. This area of the city looked nothing as it had in the seventeenth century, and to his knowledge, the residents weren't much interested in burning or drowning witches these days. That didn't stop clammy sweat from breaking out on his palms as he drove through the outskirts.

Hugh dutifully wore his KF94 mask as he returned the heavy equipment and filled out the final paperwork. This, of course, had the added benefit of obscuring his face and making it unlikely the employee would be able to give a meaningful description of him. At least, not beyond, *'It was some bloke with brown hair and brown eyes; average height, I guess.'*

Hugh had been taller than average for a thirteenth century English peasant. He was shorter than average for a twenty-first century man in the UK. 'Howard Farrington' was wearing two-inch platform shoes that obscured his true height. He was also wearing a rather ugly pair of tortoiseshell glasses. Anyone who knew Hugh de Ferrers, rough-and-ready rural blacksmith, would attest that he'd never be caught dead wearing either of those things.

He wouldn't be able to use this identity for anything else in the future, but he was confident it couldn't be easily traced back to him—not even if the investigators made it as far as interviewing heavy equipment rental businesses located over a hundred miles away from the scene of the crime.

Errand accomplished, he retrieved his van from where he'd left it in medium-term parking and drove back home. There, he spent the remainder of the day brooding over what, if anything, he should do about Philomena.

He still had no answers when he eventually collapsed on the battered sofa with a bowl of cold leftovers that probably should have been binned two days ago. He ate the stale curry without tasting it, aware that lack of sleep had finally caught up to him in a way that was becoming impossible to ignore.

Perversely, once he gave up and lay back on the sagging cushions, his brain started cycling through the past few days in an endless, repetitive loop. He stared up at the white plaster ceiling with its exposed oak beams, the evening light outside gradually fading to dusk as the hours passed. He'd always hated this particular kind of malaise — being physically exhausted while also being too mentally wound up to sleep.

Only when it was fully dark outside did weariness overcome his mind's impression of an obsessive hamster running on a wheel. He tumbled headfirst into sleep, blinking back into awareness an unknown amount of time later to find himself lying on an impossibly large and soft canopied bed — completely naked and chained to the headboard by a thin metal collar around his neck.

———————◆———————

"Whu—?" Hugh mumbled, reaching for the collar only to notice that his wrists, too, were shackled. He stared at the slender golden circlets and the ridiculous tiny chains attached to them. They resembled jewelry more than restraint, and the shackles were so finely made that the smooth metal against his skin felt somehow padded.

Candles illuminated the warm, welcoming space. A figure seated in a comfortable chair next to the bed shifted position. The movement drew Hugh's attention, and a flush of embarrassed heat rose to his face at being seen in such a predicament by another person.

Morpheus gazed at him intently, his raven's-wing brows furrowed.

"Oh," Hugh realized with a heady flash of relief. "I must be dreaming."

Hard on the heels of that realization came a second, less welcome one. Just because he was dreaming, it didn't mean this wasn't real… at least, in the sense of Morpheus actually being present with him.

Staring at him… naked and chained to an imaginary bed.

One dark brow arched, and then Morpheus' expression settled into neutral lines. "I have been awaiting your arrival. I must say, I expected you some time ago. Humans require sleep. Immortal or no, you should not push yourself so."

This seemed like an odd conversation to be having under the circumstances, with Hugh's prick on full display and enthusiastically reminding him that it still hadn't got any relief after the previous night.

"There were some things I had to take care of," he said, playing it as cool as he could manage. "The British government might not be too pleased when it finds its secret bunker sitting wide open and a dead woman inside. I needed to cover my tracks. Make sure it can't be traced back to me."

Understanding softened Morpheus' angular features. "Ah. I see." He tilted his head, assessing

Hugh. "You risked much to release me from my prison. I have not forgotten the debt I owe you."

Hugh huffed, wishing there was a handy blanket he could grab to throw over his lap. There wasn't. He was lying on top of a silken, emerald-green duvet, his head and shoulders propped up by feather pillows. There was enough slack in the chains that he supposed he could have pulled one of the pillows free and used that to hide his growing erection—but somehow the prospect felt even more humiliating than just trying to ignore it.

"You know," Hugh said, "I didn't come after you because I wanted you in my debt. You do understand that, I hope?"

"I do," Morpheus replied, in a faint tone of wonder. "However, the debt exists whether you intended it or not. I merely wish you to know that I am cognizant of it."

Hugh blinked. "Oh. Right-o, then." He cleared his throat awkwardly. "So, maybe you could tell me why I'm chained naked to your bed, in that case?"

Amusement twitched at full, sensuous lips. "I fear I am unable to assist you there. This is your dream, Hugh de Ferrers—not mine."

Hugh took that on board, until the silence in the room grew uncomfortably heavy.

"Bugger," he said.

Morpheus continued to regard him. "An interesting choice of epithet."

Hugh's face flamed hotter, at the same time his traitorous dick attempted its best imitation of a flagpole. "Erm…"

A long-fingered hand reached out, lifting the delicate gold chain attached to Hugh's right wrist as though assessing its workmanship. An instant later, a terrible thought occurred.

"Crap. *Shite*. Morpheus, I'm so sorry. They shackled you… in the bunker. I didn't mean to—" He cut himself off. Tried again. "I mean, I don't know why my brain would even come up with something like this—"

But the amusement was back again, stronger than before in the face of Hugh's floundering.

"Do you not?" Morpheus asked dryly. "You needn't concern yourself with my injured sensibilities. The shackles we choose for ourselves are entirely different than the shackles foisted on us by others."

Relief loosened the tight muscles of Hugh's shoulders. "I guess so, but still—I thought I was supposed to be the hunter here, and you were supposed to be the mysterious stag."

Morpheus stroked smooth fingers along the length of slender chain before letting it drop. "If your eternal pursuit of this unearthly white stag was meant as the gods' punishment, perhaps you have angered them by successfully catching your prize."

"And are you?" Hugh asked. "Angry?"

Morpheus' expression grew faraway. His tone became distant. "Incandescently so. About many things." His blue gaze refocused on Hugh. "None of which are related to you, my hunter."

An almost imperceptible tremor gripped Hugh's muscles—the same mingled swirl of excitement and foreboding that had vibrated within him when he'd laid a gentle hand across Morpheus' throat and pinned him to the bed in the waking world. But there was one more thing he needed to know, assuming this conversation was real, and Morpheus was truly here with him.

"Iridaceae," he said. "She disappeared at the same time you did. Is she—?"

"Healed," Morpheus replied. "I used the strength you gifted me to bring her here to the Night Lands, where I was able to repair the damage done to her physical form."

"Well," Hugh said hoarsely. "I suppose that's all right, then."

Morpheus was once again examining Hugh as though he were a fascinating and unfamiliar puzzle. "You do talk quite a bit more than I expected, given many of our... previous interactions within this plane of existence. Perhaps it was a mistake to grant you lucidity within your dreams."

Hugh swallowed hard—an audible gulp.

"I could... shut up now?" he offered meekly.

Morpheus rose from his chair, lithe as a hunting cat. Hugh's mouth went abruptly and comprehensively dry as the loose white shirt and breeches his host had been wearing melted away, dissipating like smoke in the warm candlelight to reveal the marble perfection of pale skin beneath.

"What an excellent idea," Morpheus said.

THIRTY-FIVE

Dream Interlude II

RIGHT. SO, HUGH had obviously been wrong about who was the hunter and who was the prey in this scenario. Or maybe his subconscious had known all along—since this was supposedly *his* dream.

Unfortunately, trying to untangle that particular bit of psychological fuckery was impossible when he had twelve stone of naked, chiseled godling crawling up the length of his body, caging him in place with arms and legs. Hugh's painfully hard cock brushed against something cool and equally hard as their bodies aligned, sending a jolt of heat and pleasure racing up his spine that seemed all out of proportion with the fleeting touch.

The choked squeak that lurched free of his throat in response was a sound he desperately wished to have stricken from the record. He really, *really* hoped a matching squeak hadn't emerged from his sleeping physical body, even though Baphometh would be the only one around to hear it.

"Ah," Morpheus said. "Excellent. I see now that there are other ways to curtail your loquaciousness in bed."

The God of Nightmares' face was in shadow, limned with gold from behind by the candlelight. Hugh glared up at him, nonetheless. "You're the one using words like *loquaciousness* and *curtail* in bed! And you call *me*—"

The words cut off in a low-pitched whine as hands glided down his flanks. Smooth thumbs traced the dips above his hipbones, drawing an urgent throb from his dick. The problem was, Morpheus *hadn't moved* his hands. They still rested on the impossibly soft mattress next to Hugh's shoulders.

Morpheus tilted his head, considering his captive with an air of dry amusement. "Why so surprised, little hunter? You are in *my* realm now."

Hugh blinked up at him. Ghostly stag's antlers framed Morpheus' wild mop of dark hair, ever so slightly out of phase with the rest of him. Both *there* and *not there*.

Then one of the invisible hands slid down to grasp Hugh's prick, stroking him from root to tip, and every single thought fled his consciousness with an audible *whoosh* of receding air.

"*Fuck*," he choked out, abruptly on the verge of coming.

The *hand-that-wasn't* receded, leaving him teetering on the brink, his balls pulled up tight to his body as they readied to spend.

"You should not have waited so long to come to me," Morpheus said—and while Hugh couldn't *see* the supercilious slant of a dark brow in the dim light, he could hear it clearly enough behind the words.

"If I'd known what was waiting for me, I'd have been here five minutes after you left," Hugh managed.

Morpheus made a low noise of male satisfaction and shifted position, nudging Hugh's thighs apart with his knees until he was resting his hips between them. "Good answer."

Somehow, a cushion had appeared beneath Hugh's arse, lifting his pelvis a few inches off the bed. The invisible hands returned to their work, only now there was one squeezing the base of his cock while another delved behind his balls. Two more stroked through his chest hair, teasing his nipples until he squirmed and gasped in reaction.

A ghostly finger circled his hole, which had mysteriously grown slick despite the utter absence of lube. The finger pressed in, slipping inside his body easily. *Too* easily. A different kind of pleasure flared, like sparks of lightning skittering to life along Hugh's nerve endings. A second finger joined the first, smoothly and painlessly, followed soon after by a third. Hugh arched and swallowed a cry at the delicious stretch, because *how*—? It had been *years*...

You are in my realm now.

The words echoed in his mind. A dream... this was all a dream. His body accepted the intrusion effortlessly because he wished it to, or perhaps because Morpheus did.

Hugh clenched his teeth and thrust his hips into the pressure, seeking more—rationality fleeing in the face of animal need too long denied.

"Please," he rasped. "Please, please, please..."

Morpheus made another approving noise and shifted position slightly. The nonexistent fingers dissolved, replaced a moment later by a *very* existent blunt cockhead. Its velvet skin was eerily cool against Hugh's overheated flesh. Then Morpheus pushed inside him with an air of possession.

For an instant, Hugh thought that single, inexorable slide might be the best thing he'd ever felt in eight hundred years. That was until slick, invisible tightness enveloped Hugh's cock—as though Hugh was somehow simultaneously doing to Morpheus everything that Morpheus was doing to him.

He gasped with the perfect, overwhelming impossibility of it.

The moment the constriction at the base of Hugh's dick disappeared, he was a goner—thrusting wildly back and forth between the sensation of taking and being taken. Once, twice, three times, and his climax flooded outward, spilling over in a white-hot explosion of feeling that jerked through his body in pulsing waves.

Countless unseen hands gentled him through it, stroking and petting. When his final shudders subsided, he lay panting like an exhausted hunting hound, staring open-mouthed at the ethereal, antlered creature poised above him.

Morpheus lifted one of his actual hands, balancing on the other as he stroked his thumb over Hugh's lower lip.

"A very promising start, my hunter," he murmured, and began to move inside Hugh again with slow, rolling strokes.

Hugh made a noise that sounded like "*Guh,*" and lay trembling beneath him, his dick remaining stubbornly erect as the impossible double fucking lifted him ever-upward toward an equally impossible second orgasm.

Dream world, he remembered dizzily, falling headfirst into the all-encompassing sensation with the air of someone who never wanted to wake up.

Despite the marble coolness of the body moving against his, Hugh felt warm in a way that he hadn't since he'd lain curled together with his long-lost wife so long ago, with the sun dappling the ground around them as it filtered through the branches of the ancient oak at the edge of the commons.

Absolute safety.

Absolute belonging.

He only realized tears had gathered behind his eyes when he clenched them shut beneath the force of his second climax; moisture squeezing out to roll down his temples. This time, Morpheus stilled above him when Hugh was finished, as though sensing that anything more would be too much.

Hugh couldn't bring himself to open his eyes. He swallowed hard, feeling the faint constriction of the gold collar around his throat as his Adam's apple bobbed.

"Don't... don't leave me," he whispered, though he hadn't meant to say the words aloud. They came without his permission, spilling from his lips in a rush. "Please don't disappear on me. Not again. I don't think I could—"

He managed to bite down on the tail of the painful admission, cutting it off, though the damage had already been done.

Silence settled over the sumptuous room, slicing into Hugh's heart like a blade. Like a bullet.

Between one breath and the next, Hugh was no longer shackled to the bed, sticky and sweating, with a cock up his arse and invisible hands stroking him. Instead, he was clean and cozy, tucked under the covers with his head resting on a wiry shoulder. Fingers carded the hair back from his temple in an idle rhythm.

"You are safe here, my dreamer," Morpheus said, in a tone Hugh had never heard him use before. "You must wake eventually—but I would be a poor lover to reward such constancy with further abandonment."

Hugh's breath tripped. All his defenses had been stripped away in this place of the mind, leaving him terrifyingly bare. The conversation could only have happened in dreams. In the real world, he would never have let his walls fall to rubble like this. Here, those walls no longer existed. There was no filter between his subconscious and the man—the *god*—curled in the bed next to him.

"Lover? We're lovers now?" he echoed, aware of how foolish it sounded after the past twenty-four hours.

Morpheus let a breath out through his nose. His fingers in Hugh's hair stilled.

"If you wish it to be so. There are... complications to such an arrangement," he said, with evident reluctance. "Being the *concubinus* of a god—even a minor one—is not without its dangers. Especially now, when I am vulnerable, and my domain is in chaos."

Hugh sat up, ignoring the protests of his limp, exhausted muscles. "Your domain. The... Night Lands? Is that right? Is that where we are?"

Morpheus met his gaze. "I am in the Night Lands. You are dreaming. Your body remains in the Sublunary, safely asleep." He gave his head a small shake. "The point is, by associating yourself with me in such an overt manner, you may draw the wrong kind of attention at a time when I am in a poor position to defend you from possible harm."

Hugh frowned, thinking of Phobetor. Thinking of humanity slowly going mad, and of horses' legs jerking in terrorized spasms as they slept a tortured, restless sleep.

"Morpheus," he said. "The human world is fucked up beyond belief right now. War, plague, genocide, madness—is this because you were held prisoner for so long?"

His companion turned half away, his blue eyes growing distant. "Some of it. Vast numbers of my oneiri are missing from the Night Lands. They are the creatures that craft nightmares and dreams. Iridaceae says many of them have followed my brother to the waking world, after he promised them free rein to spread terror outside of the tightly controlled realm of mortal sleep. I cannot allow such a situation to continue unaddressed."

Hugh watched him in profile, letting this new information sink in. There was no question in his mind which brother Morpheus was referencing.

"If you're going to war against Phobetor," he said, "then you'll need allies. Other people at your back." He thought of the God of Fear's terrible, piercing eyes, cutting into him in a London alley in 1721. He thought of the crippling terror he'd felt. He imagined Morpheus facing that same opponent alone. "Let me be one of those people."

Morpheus turned to look at him directly again. Their gazes locked for a long moment, bridging the gap between waking and sleeping, humanity and the divine.

"You would be wiser to flee while you have the chance," Morpheus said.

Hugh cocked an eyebrow at him. "Flee where? Two of your brothers already know who I am. Let's just say, I think I'm on your family's radar whether I stick around or not." Heat rose to his cheeks as he remembered Phantasos laughing at him as he shifted back from Morpheus' form to his own.

Morpheus looked troubled, but he nodded. "I suppose I should expect nothing less from you. There was a reason I chose you as my champion, these many years ago."

That was another can of worms entirely, but not one Hugh felt able to delve into right now.

"So, it wasn't my rugged good looks?" he joked weakly.

Morpheus pursed his lips, a small smile hiding at the edges of the expression. "It was not. Your rugged good looks are merely a happy bonus. I chose you for your empathy, your fidelity, your fearlessness in the defense of those you care about—"

"Stop," Hugh begged, not willing to hear the words in a place where he had no barriers against them. "Let's… just pretend it was my looks, all right?" He cleared his throat. "How about a guided tour of this *domain* of yours, eh? That seems like a good place to start."

"As you wish," Morpheus said. He rose from the bed, clothing reforming around his lithe form as he did so. One graceful hand reached out to Hugh — an invitation.

Hugh looked down to find that a loose shirt and breeches had draped themselves around his body as well. "Neat trick, that," he said, swinging his legs over the edge of the mattress.

For eight hundred years, the little flame of hope for the future that lived inside Hugh's heart had been both his beacon and his curse. Now, it flared higher, throwing off fragile light and warmth.

Hope for himself.

Hope for the two of them.

Hope for humanity and the waking world.

Hugh took the offered hand and rose, ready to follow the God of Nightmares and Dreams into his kingdom — evil brothers, political plots, and unknown celestial dangers be damned.

finis

Morpheus and Hugh's adventure continues in
Book Two: *Sublunary.*

To discover more books by this author, visit
www.rasteffan.com